WHEN CIRCLES END

WHEN CIRCLES END

JACQUELINE O'HARA

TATE PUBLISHING
AND ENTERPRISES, LLC

When Circles End

Published by Tate Publishing & Enterprises, LLC
127 E. Trade Center Terrace | Mustang, Oklahoma 73064 USA
1.888.361.9473 | www.tatepublishing.com

Tate Publishing is committed to excellence in the publishing industry. The company reflects the philosophy established by the founders, based on Psalm 68:11,
"The Lord gave the word and great was the company of those who published it."

Cover design by Jan Sunday Quilaquil
Interior design by Honeylette Pino

Published in the United States of America

ISBN: 978-1-62902-047-1
1. Fiction / Action & Adventure
2. Fiction / Coming of Age
13.10.01

DEDICATION

To the amazing teachers I've had over the years for helping me become the writer I am today, and to my loving family and amazing friends who stand by me no matter what.

CHELSEY O'NEIL

Cheerleading captain, incredibly smart, and undeniably pretty would be how I, Chelsey O'Neil, would describe the pure awesomeness that is me. I have bright blond hair, light blue eyes, a smooth completion, and am five feet and eight inches. Some people think of me as a taller version of Barbie; of course, I'm way smarter than her, at least that's what Trina says. FYI, she's my BFF.

Trina's like the twin sister I never had and always wanted. She looks like we could be identical twins; we look identical from our blond hair to our perfectly manicured toes. The only thing that's different about us is that she can play sports like nobody I've ever seen; you tell her how to play, and the minute she gets on the field, it looks like she has played all her life. Now her favorite sport is track because most of the time she doesn't have to rely on other people to help her win. She really doesn't care much for the playing, but she would run to the ends of the earth to win.

Think that sums up everything, at least leaving out that I am sixteen in thirteen days. My birthday is on the eighteenth and I can almost feel myself in those comfy tan leather seats, adjusting my mirrors just so, so I can see the road and can check my makeup at the same time; hey, a girl's got high expectations.

Back to my daydream. Now where am I? Oh, yes, checking my mirrors, revving the engine like a street racer would do. I could almost hear the sweet purr of the engine and feel the cool wind brushing past me as I go sixty miles an hour in my soon-to-be red convertible Ferrari. How did I know I was getting a Ferrari? Well, let's just say my parents were never really good at putting documents away; and well, my sister and I have never really been good at minding our own business. The end.

So now that I have given you a short sum of my achievements, and a bit about me, I will get to the story, the other story. I know, I know. You would probably rather like listening about me, but for your own safety, I will bore you with my other story. And to some of those insanely picky readers who stop reading after the first couple of pages if they don't like it or sounds too scary, they should consider changing their habits right about now since this is something everyone needs to hear… like it or not.

So now I'm sounding all solemn and probably kind of freaky, but I'm just preparing you for what this book is going to throw at you—BTW, I'm not responsible for you being admitted to a nuthouse, you wetting your pants, or having nightmares, etc.

Now, in my experience with all of this, I have learned two very essential lessons. One, don't ask questions you don't want to know the answer to, and two, never steal a bait car…but I will get to all of that, eventually.

So here I am sitting happily on this rather uncomfortable bus seat reminding myself that it won't be much longer. Soon I will never have to ride a bus again. It feels too early to be a Thursday, and I keep having this feeling we are going to have a pop quiz in History today, but still I wore my usual happy grin and proceeded to look out the window, watching people running or walking their dogs.

The bus ride was a blur, and before I can even remember to grab my lunch, I am pushed out the door…I am a bit of a daydreamer. Realizing I won't be having lunch unless I somehow got ten bucks, I start shuffling through my purse praying that I remembered to bring some cash; cell phone, no. receipts, no. pens, no.

"Come on, where are you!" I say to my purse in frustration.

"Well, I was right behind you," says Chase Maxwell with his infamous half grins that make my knees turn to jelly; okay, being off topic, his name is so cool, like it fits him in that way. I don't know how to describe it. But it's definitely hot. Let's keep it at that.

Chase is taller than me by like four inches and has a kind of stylish punk rock getup that looks like an easy took-me-five-minutes kind of style, starting with long wavy dark brown hair, which hangs just below his eyebrows, and swoops to the left, looking stylishly casual. After that, he has white high-top sneakers that have black and silver trim. Then he has trendy dark skinny jeans with chains dangling from his belt loop, his jeans go low on his waist and end on the top of his killer shoes. Matching his jeans, he has a vintage Beatles V-neck 100 percent cotton T-shirt on and a thin leather jacket that hugs the bulges of his arm muscles, which makes him look the perfect type of buff—like not body builder buff (which is kind of creepy) but like enough where he looks totally in shape and handsome—he almost looks Photoshopped he's so cute.

"Oh, didn't see you there…I was talking to my purse. It's being very difficult," I say blushing, but I give my bag a scolding glare to prove my point, which earns me a playful laugh.

"Well, if anyone can kick a purse into shape, it's you," he says playing along, which is true, I am a miracle worker on the side. I avert my eyes from his strong arms and try to focus on those stunning gray eyes, which isn't too much trouble because everything about this guy is irresistible. I'm surprised he only has half the school falling over him

"Yeah, well I'll believe that when it coughs up my ten bucks," I say a bit grumpily, which I regret the minute it leaves my lips

"Oh, well, I got to head to class…Will I see you at the game?" he asks, trying to change the subject, of course, the minute you bring money into the mix the cute guys go running.

"Yeah, wait, is that tonight?" I ask with a start. How could I forget? It's the biggest baseball game they will have all season! It's us against THS, Timber High School, our biggest rivals from debate teams to baseball teams; they beat us every year, stupid private school. But, now that Chase has joined the team (since he already played every sport in the whole world, I guess he found some time for baseball now too) we might actually have a chance…for once.

"Yeah, it starts at six…Why, do you have somewhere else to be?" he asks quizzically

"No! Of course not, I just…never mind. We got to get to class. See you later?" I ask, my turn avoiding a topic

"Yeah…Okay, see you later then," he says, giving me a look that reads, "*I know you're avoiding this conversation, and if you can't make it just tell me, but I won't push you further*" with those gorgeous eyes. He turns and strolls away. It's amazing how much a guy can talk without actually talking, so precise, and at the same time it's so very annoying.

But in truth, I got stuck babysitting my little sister Emma, the most annoying ten-year-old ever in existence. Does that sound harsh? Well it should because now I will either look like an idiot having to watch my sister and go to the game or not go to the game and find a better excuse about why I didn't just bring her…Life can be so difficult at times.

"Ring, ring!" screeches the late bell.

"Oh, crap!" I say to myself quietly this time, not wanting another odd conversation. "I'm late!" I hurry in still halfheartedly digging through my purse. *Well, less calories would be good for me*, I think, trying to bring up my mood as I make my way to my seat in the middle of the class.

It's really the best place to be, it says, *I am a good student and I want to learn*, without portraying teacher's pet, aka the class kiss up. That and the seat doesn't say: *Hopefully if I sit in back, I won't be called on as much!* Either, see? The perfect in between!

"Ah, Miss O'Neil, you're late…Care to explain?" says my stupid history teacher Mr. Martin, stopping me in my tracks

"Oh, um…well…" I stumble on my words looking for a reasonable excuse. "Well, I lost track of time and got pushed off the bus before I could grab my lunch, and well, I was trying to get some money from my purse… and it's not cooperating very well right now, and—" Mr. Martin interrupts my excessive rambling with an annoyed look holding up his hand signaling stop.

"Miss O'Neil, this is the fourth time you've been late to my class…this week! Now if you would like to avoid a trip to the principal's office, I suggest you sit down and be on time tomorrow and next week as well…capiche?" he finishes still with a sour expression, averting his eyes from me to glare at the class who were trying to suppress their silly giggles and smirks.

Mr. Martin is an older man with a receding hairline. He has light brown hair that almost looks blond in the light; it was always combed back with enough gel to stop a bullet—even though he really doesn't have enough hair to use gel in my opinion—he has small, round looks like there's no color at all, just white eyes with black pupils; it looks really creepy even after I've been in his class for a while now.

He is tall—maybe, like if he were to stand straight, instead of all hunched over— he also has a long pointed nose and large rectangular glasses that he seems to always be pushing back up his big ole nose, and he always talks as if he were in a library, even the first row struggles to hear at times.

His attire looks like something a nerd would wear in the seventies. That, and he wears the same thing every day: coffee-brown long trousers that just hardly reach his ankles. Along with the pants, he has matching brown suspenders with a beige button-up shirt, and some type of checkered bow tie. In the left-hand breast pocket he has three colored pens: *red, blue, and yellow. I've got the primary colors!* he would say in that deep crackly voice of his.

Right now I need some major kiss-up points, especially since at the moment it's been one, two, three…four strikes? I'm surprised that at three strikes I wasn't…out. Yeah, I'm still on the whole baseball thing, which is kind of funny because I hate baseball—in the nicest way possible—and the only reason I actually know the game is because of Chase Maxwell, just thinking about him brought a smile to my face, and apparently, my mind was away from the class because all of a sudden I hear, "Do you understand Miss O'Neil?" from Mr. Martin, and if I had a dollar, I would bet that he is definitely not happy.

"Umm…Yes, Mr. Martin, sorry again," I say, snapping out of my daydream.

"Well, you can sit now," he says, nodding towards a chair in the front.

"Oh yeah…sorry," I say, forgetting that I was still standing. Wow, I must look so bizarre right now. I walk as fast as I can without breaking into a run and sit down in the seat that Mr. Martin pointed to.

"Let my worst nightmare begin," I mumble under my breath as I take my seat and pull out my textbook a pen and my notebook from my cluttered purse.

"Like I was saying before this last interruption," he continued to talk, but I am totally blanking, zoning out. Something is seriously up this last week. I can't help it, and normally, I was never like this. *I must not be getting enough sleep or something*, I think to myself trying to shake off all the daydreams and focus.

Somehow I get through school without being called on once, that's pretty lucky since I wasn't paying attention to anything, even if Kim Kardashian herself were to have come into our class I wouldn't have noticed. Finally, I snap out of my trance when I walk off the bus. The first thing I do is check the time; three thirty, that's two and a half hours till Chase's game, and plenty of time to find someone to sit the little brat.

After an hour and a half of calling sitting companies and friends, I call up Trina hoping she would do it because she was my last hope if I wanted to see Chase.

"Please! Please watch her. It's only for a couple of hours. I already promised Chase I would be at the game!" I say to Trina over the phone. There was a long silence on the other end. Then a deep sigh. *Oh, please let her say yes, please!* I think to myself, closing my eyes so tightly that I say little spots on the inside of my eyelids.

"Fine, but only for a few hours, then I'm out of there if you are there or not," she says with authority.

"Thank you so, so, so, so, so—"

"Hey, what are sisters for anyway?" she says a bit more cheerful than before.

"Well, I don't know about my little brat of a sister, but you're the best sister I could ever ask for!" I say, obviously pleasing her, so I add, "Do you think you could drop me off at the game? I still can't drive." I say this in a small voice expecting her to explode but instead says, "Yeah, okay sure, but I swear if you and Chase don't hit it off—"

"Ugh! But I need to be there by six, so could you hurry up it's five thirty, and it takes thirty minutes to get down there."

"Sure, I'll be there in five minutes," she says, and I could just picture her face laughing happily as she speeds down the back roads because, following the speed limit, it would take about fifteen minutes to get to my house without any traffic. I hear a click on the other end, and I know the conversation is over.

"Okay, now I just have to break the news to the little brat," I say to myself, walking down the spiral staircase.

"EMMA!" I scream when I'm halfway down.

"What?" she yells back annoyed.

"I'm going to the game. Trina is coming to watch you," I say, thinking of all she could do to make my life chaotic.

"I don't need a babysitter!" she yells up to me.

"I know! She's just coming over to um...watch TV, but she's older than you, so listen to her okay?" I say, knowing that if I protest she will turn green and muscled, and I would end up picking up after the little hulk.

"Fine...Wait, does Mom know about this?" she asks when I reach her in the living room. She had a devilish grin that only Satan himself could've made.

"No, but I have ten bucks on the counter to buy your silence," I say, keeping my eyes on hers.

"Well, look at the time my movie marathon is on, looks like I will be in my room for three and a half hours. Don't forget to watch me," she says. Yes, that's enough time!

"Okay, be a good little monster and stay in your room, and Alexander Hamilton is yours," I say, already grabbing my coat. *Where is Trina?* I think to myself right as the door opens to Trina.

"By the way, that took at least ten minutes," I say, giving Trina a hard time.

"Yeah, got a little sidetracked I guess. Let's go," she says without any emotion on her face; something seemed a bit off about her today. *But maybe it's what I have been going through*, I counter myself. And off we go.

Surprisingly, we get there in record time and only missed like five minutes of the game.

"Thank you so much!" I say happily. I hug her awkwardly in the car, and I open the door ready to get out.

"Chelsey O'Neil," says Trina almost robotically.

"Yeah, Trina…Is everything all right?" I ask, concern gripping at the back of my neck, and I don't know if I was just overreacting, but I swear I saw her eyes turn red like full on entire eye red, like no pupil. It was only a second, but I could've sworn they did.

"Trina? Are you feeling okay?" I ask, fear replacing the concern I once had. That's of course when she grabs my hand—and it wasn't like a "hold on, don't forget your purse!" No, it was like, "I want to kill you" death grip—I look at her stunned, yet she had no emotion on her face.

"Okay, um, Trina? I'm going to go now," I say, terrified when she doesn't loosen her grip. I work my nails into her hands, no use. So I try pulling her hair, yet she sits unmoving, unblinking.

"Stop, you're hurting me!" I say, tears brimming in my eyes. "What are you doing?" I ask feeling threatened, betrayed.

"Chelsey O'Neil!" she screams at me like some sick robot. It was not her voice that's for sure, and it was scratchy and cold.

"Let go!" I scream one last time and rip my arm from her grasp, and then I turn and run.

Now knowing that the only sport I do is shopping, and Trina's broken more than one school record in this category, I knew I wouldn't have much time. I run faster than ever before, ditching my high heels as I go. The only sounds I can hear is the air rushing by my ears, and the loud huffing of my breath. Wow, I feel out of shape—thanks for nothing, stupid pilates. Yet I knew I was going way faster than normal, especially since I closed a five minute walk in only five seconds... But that's impossible.... right?

The game started, and no one was even looking my way. I look for a place I could hide. *Under the bleachers!* I think, already exhausted.

I duck into the bleachers praying she didn't see me come here. On my hands and knees, I feel my way through, occasionally coming across some garbage or something sticky. So gross! It's dark out, and it feels like I'm encased in a smelly damp and moldy storm cellar.

"Hey watch it!" says a voice, and believe me, I screamed so loud; I'm surprised that they didn't hear me over the cheering.

"Stop it! You're going to draw attention to us," he says in a hush tone, but I heard a mix of fear and annoyance on his voice.

"Who are you?" I ask not hearing any evil robot in the mix, but you can never be too careful, right?

The mysterious boy gives a sigh as if it pains him to give up his identity.

"Josh...Josh Williams," he says reluctantly. I almost laughed out loud.

"Josh Williams?" I exclaim, now normally I wouldn't have ever known him; he was more of the "keep to myself and blend" kind of guy. But when my history grades started dropping, I had to seek the help of a nerd but not one that will laugh to all his friends; I needed someone secluded from the rest of the high school drama, and so, I needed Josh Williams. But personally, I didn't think he was *this* much of a...well, nobody!

"Hello, Chelsey," he says in an exaggerated sigh. *Wait, how did he know it was me?* And that's exactly what I asked.

"Because you have the highest, most shrill voice I've ever heard," he replies curtly and at that I was speechless.

"You, you I—" I am interrupted by him rudely putting his hand over my mouth, so as punishment, I bite him, hard.

"OW!" he exclaims, pulling his hand away.

"Should teach you, you little…little…" I falter at a loss for words, probably for the first time in my life, what was he?

"Little, what?" I hear him say smugly. He was being so annoying! But just then some light reveals his features more clearly, his hair was dirty and messy, and his face looked gruesome in the pale red light. Did… did he have a black eye? I stare at him in wonderment.

"Josh, what happened to you?" I ask stupefied.

"You're stupid boyfriend happened," he says, angrily clenching his teeth.

"What boyfriend? Oh, do you mean Chase?" I ask bewildered and slightly happy that some people think we're together. But back to the matter at hand.

"Well, *Chase* is a bit of a bully if you haven't noticed already," he says through gritted teeth.

"Chase is not a bully! He is incredibly kind, you're lying!" I say loudly.

"Does my face lie!" he says, turning his head so I could get a better look at his bruise; it looked painful for sure, no wonder he was in a bad mood.

"Then what happened?" I exclaim, seething.

"I didn't give your little pal the grade he wanted on his last paper, that should explain itself," he said, his eyes focusing on me with indescribable intensity. That's when I see something shiny in the corner of his eye. He swipes at it before I can really focus on it, but I know what it was, and I also know he wasn't lying. I just can't believe Chase could be so cruel; Chase seemed so smart and charming.

"I'm sorry," I say, quietly feeling guilty.

"Why are you apologizing? You don't even care if I'm alive!" he says cruelly. *But I do! I am a person too!* I wanted to tell him, but in truth, I never really cared about Josh's social life other than what he was doing for me. And that realization was the worst part of it all.

"Look, I get why you would be mad," I begin, but before I can even apologize, I notice that the red light was getting brighter and brighter, I feel a hand on my ankle—a grip that I knew all too well. I look back and see Trina with no emotion at all, and bright red eyes.

"Josh, help!" I scream, but when I look back to where he is, I'm so shocked from what I see. There was Josh with something over his mouth; someone was holding it there, and I wasn't sure if the person was trying to kill him or help him. Wait, is he breathing? I struggle against Trina to get a better look at the mystery person, and it's…it's Chase…and he has red eyes too.

I know, I'm not exactly the hero type, but what could I have done? Josh was…I don't know. But I couldn't help him either way because Trina had her little death grip on me. If I had to die, I didn't want to see it coming. So in the end, I faint. Yep, I'm Chelsey O'Neil, the brave girl who fainted.

JOSH WILLIAMS

Okay, here it goes. My name is Josh Williams, and I'm what you might call a nobody. In my mind, nobodies are people who still haven't found their clique, kind of like how you don't know what you want to be when you grow up, till you actually grow up. Unfortunately to other people, nobodies are the weird kooky people—which is so not true—so in the meantime, I stick to myself, keep my grades up, and other people's grades up. And when it's all over, and I've survived high school, it'll be my time to shine. And believe me, that day can't come soon enough.

I'm tall and skinny, not exactly the muscle head that everyone fawns over. I also have shaggy black hair and sea-green eyes. I have a long almost oval face to match my tall stature, and to top off the whole thing, I'm pale as a ghost even when it's one hundred degrees outside. I don't burn; I don't tan. I stay my white scrawny self.

"Good morning, sunshine, the earth says hello," says my sister in that fake gentleness she is so good at.

"What do you want?" I demand, realizing she's in my room; and my room, plus little sister, equals something's up, or she wants something. Either way, I never win.

"Oh nothing, sweet brother of mine," she says, her voice like velvet. I would never admit this, but her voice actually sounds pretty.

"Cut to the chase here," I say, still waking up; it was too early to succumb to her little act.

"Okay, can you do my math homework? I'm falling behind, and Mom's about to pop a gasket," she says in a begging tone. So I knew I wouldn't stand a chance at saying no, but I could at least make her beg a little more.

"What's in it for me?" I sneer joyfully.

"Well, I could give you a coupon for a spray tan. You look a little pale," she begins insensitively, "or I could give you a makeover so the jocks at your school don't beat you up as much, and that right there is a really big job," she continues snottily.

"Okay, okay, I get it," I say, my blood boiling from her insults. "And just for that, no!"

"Come on, please! You already do like five other peoples' homework, just this once, for me, your sister!" she says, her smooth voice more edgy this time. She was really upset, huh?

"Fine," I say, acknowledging that this probably isn't how to solve a problem, but I couldn't help it. Don't ask why, but my sister had a way of getting what she wanted, and she's only in eighth grade. It's not that hard of math anyway, "But this means you owe me one, got that?" I ask knowing I'll probably never use it; it's more of an ego thing anyway.

"Great, here...It's due tomorrow," she says, handing me a thin packet.

"Wow, your teacher is like the homework Nazi, huh?" I say, surprised at the daily load of homework.

"Can you do it?" she asks, a hint of concern in her voice.

"Yeah, yeah, it'll be done by tonight. I will work on it at study hall," I say, waving off her concern.

"Good, oh, and do you want me to make up for the homework thing?" she asks almost innocently. I squint at her as if I'm trying to read her mind.

"Umm, sure, why not?" I say, thinking it will be something like, "Don't wear your pj's to school, or comb your hair, it looks like you got electrocuted."

"You're going to be late in fifteen minutes," she says with a genuine smile and slips out of my room. I frantically try to find a clock to validate her claim…and there on my phone read:

6:55
Thursday, April 5

"Come on!" I yell in frustration. I take a couple deep breaths. "It'll be okay, I'll be okay," I repeat to myself over and over again while I pick through some clothes to wear.

Now, I'm not really that worried about a tardy showing up on my report card. But what I am worried about is Chase Maxwell; he's the biggest muscle head of them all. He does every sport you can think of—football, lacrosse, soccer, track, basketball, and now baseball. And the worst thing about him, he's dumb as a stump; and in most cases, that would be an insult to stumps! But unfortunately, the school makes all athletes keep a C+ average, or else, no school sports for them. And if you still don't get it, he needs someone to keep it up for him; and unfortunately, being the lonely genius that I am, I fit the bill.

So how does this make me afraid of being late? Well, since Chase will walk in right as the bell rings, I normally get to school twenty minutes early, you know so I don't bump into him 'cause he can be a bit… grumpy in the morning. And since I'm such a geek, I have this plan with my science teacher Mrs. Jackson; so in the morning. I come early and help prepare the room and clean the class equipment.

Not today of course. I get dressed in a hurry and give my hair a quick comb through while gargling with some mouthwash, knowing it's as close to a toothbrush as I can get right now in this current time crunch. I pack my textbooks in a hurry and run out the door, convincing myself that if I were there right on time, Chase couldn't do anything to me in front of other people…still it felt as if freezing water ran through my veins as my heart beat in my ears.

It only takes me a minute to get to the school since I live in the neighborhood adjacent to it, and I was there a few minutes early, lucky for me Chase was talking to Chelsey O'Neil (a popular girl I tutor, and occasionally do homework for) when I arrive; figures, the stupidest—but buffest—guys get the stupidest—but prettiest—girls. I don't really care as long as I can avoid Chase till I get into class. I'm still watching him when he looks up. We look at each other for half a second. I start to pick up my pace. *Got to get inside*, I think as Chase starts to stride towards me. *Oh god, I'm dead*, I think furiously, but thankfully, I'm submersed in the crowd of students. *Time to get to class.*

I rush into class out of breath, heart beating a mile a minute. Placing my backpack on the back of my chair, I try to calm down to focus on the lesson, but I can't help it, my mind keeps drifting to Chase.

I already know he's upset at the last report I wrote for him. It was a time crunch, sure. But I knew it only needed to be a C+, so I slacked a little; he should be doing this on his own anyway. sometimes, I need to know when it's a good time to dump his grade.

I keep thinking of all the things I should say, all the things that will happen the next time we meet, I know I can't avoid him forever...but I just feel like if I avoid him long enough he will forget the whole thing. Just thinking about this gets me through the first half of the day.

Lunch—it's the place where friends sit together, and you can eat while watching idiots deck each other trying to show their macho-ness. Who doesn't like lunch! Today, I sneak out the door to the courtyard trying to get away from the crowds where Chase normally hangs out. And while I'm eating my turkey sandwich innocently, Chase appears in front of me with an angry expression. *I'm going to die*, I think, gripping the sides of my jeans in anticipation

"So a C- is really pulling my grade, bro," he says mildly with fierce eyes piercing into mine.

"That was unfairly graded. It...It should've been at least a C+ easily. I guess I just forgot how hard a grader your teacher is," I say, hoping I can get away unscathed—at least I hoped.

"Huh, accident, right?" he says with a crooked smile.

"Yeah, a total mistake," I say, nodding my head vigorously; my knuckles are turning white from gripping so intensely.

"Well, okay then," he starts with a smile. *Wow, maybe I have thought of Chase all wrong*, I think relaxing just a bit, my fingers were already thanking me.

"Hey, come here, I want to show you something," he says with a charismatic smile. Although I hesitate, I move to where he's standing.

"What is it?" I ask confused, then my lower abdomen explodes with pain; and before I can react, his fists connect with my jaw with a sickening crunch. I try to punch him in the nose with a weak fist, but he dodges it like a pro and pops me square in the face with quick efficient and painful jabs. Staggering, I swipe at my nose, regretting it after another rain of pain sears across my face. *Jeez, does he take boxing too?* I think, staggering backwards. A crimson streak is on my long sleeved shirt where I had wiped at.

"Come on, don't you know how to fight? No? Well then, this will be good for you," he says, happily bouncing on the balls of his feet, like a cat ready to strike.

"Stop...please," I say weakly feeling wrecked. Why hadn't anyone tried to stop him? Not even a teacher? I felt defeated; my face felt like it got smashed by a truck, and my abdomen didn't feel much better.

"This'll teach you not to mess with me," he says through an evil smile, and I can't reply, I really can't reply. My jawbone feels disconnected from my face; I feel something moist roll down my cheek, and I wince as the salty tears sting the open sores on my smashed face. "Oh, don't act like a baby," he says to me angrily.

I take a step back, holding up my hands, trying to signal that I don't want to fight, a truce. Unfortunately, he didn't get the memo; he takes two large strides, and he's on top of me. His strong muscular arm rises as if to finish me off. *He probably only wants one last blow*, I think. *Either way, playing dead wouldn't be a bad idea.* My mind continues to race with possibilities.

Closing my eyes, I'm bracing myself for pain. But no pain came; I start to relax a little, but don't open my eyes just yet. When pain still doesn't come, I look up to see Chase looking furious. He raises his arm again, but this time, I don't close my eyes. And as I watch, his fist flies at me with superhuman force; but before it reaches me, it starts to slow, and slow, till it stops only centimeters from my face. I'm too sore to flinch, but I knew on the inside I was. I could see he was really trying to hit me, but his hand and my face didn't connect, as if held apart by some type of magnetic force field... could I be doing this?

"What the—" he shouts angrily, turning twenty-seven different shades of red, flashing me a murderous look and lifts his arm again, but I don't want to push my luck, so I run. Well it was more of a limp, but Chase doesn't seem to be following, at least if he were, he would've killed me by now.

With that thought, I limp as fast as I can, and go to the only place I can think of—Mrs. Jackson's science class. Normally she eats lunch in her room, and I know it's the only place Chase won't look, now that I think about it, I don't know why I didn't go there in the first place. *But she'll help. I know she will.* I make my way up the hall, starting to feel the full extent of my injuries, and occasionally looking over my shoulder to make sure he wasn't following me.

Finally I see the door, and not wanting to intrude, I knock as hard as I can. The door opens to a girl, about my age, and she looks vaguely familiar, but I couldn't match her with a name. It didn't really matter because I pass out the minute she opens the door, falling into her arms.

"Josh, Josh! Are you okay?" says a familiar voice.

"Um, well, I feel like I'm dead. Does that count as okay?" I ask sarcastically.

"Well, you're obviously well enough for sarcasm. I say you'll live. What about you, Valery?" says Mrs. Jackson, giving me one of her motherly smiles. That's why Mrs. Jackson's my favorite teacher, because she really brings her class to life; it's more like we talk eye to eye rather than teacher to student.

"Yeah, he'll live," says someone over to my right; I look over to see the same girl who answered the door.

"Oh, I don't believe we've met. I'm Josh Williams," I say, trying to get up for her to shake my hand, but I'm stopped by an extreme ripping pain through my whole body.

"Slowly!" she yelps and gently pushes me down back into a lying position. Her touch feels so feathery light; for a brief second, all my pain ebbs, and I feel energy circulating through me. But as she takes her hand away, my pain hits me again with full force, making my head swirl. I'm lying on two tables pushed together with someone's jacket under my head.

"Thanks," I say through the pain, gritting my teeth so I don't scream.

"No problem," she says, giving me a smile full of colorful braces. "My name is Valery Jackson."

"Wait, did you say—"

"Yeah, I'm Samantha Jackson's daughter," says Valery, interrupting me midthought.

"Wait…so your Mrs. Jackson's daughter?" I start like an idiot. *Of course she is, she just told me!* I think, feeling stupid. "So do you go to this school? I…I…um, don't remember seeing you before," I ask continuing to talk like a babbling idiot. "What grade?" I continue while trying to remember anytime where I had seen her before.

"Yeah, I go here, and this week my teachers decided it would be best for me to skip a grade, so it can be more challenging for me and all…so I'm in your grade starting Monday," she says in a quiet voice.

Valery is my kind of pretty, no makeup or tight clothing. She had light brown hair that framed her round face; she also has thin naturally red lips and is average height. She was wearing a simple baby blue button-up shirt with the sleeves rolled up to her elbow and worn jeans and running shoes. Her brown eyes have little gold shards that are just barely noticeable but are mesmerizing to look at. There's no doubt that she's going to look like her mom when she is older;

she already did a little. She seemed natural, so nice and apparently very smart; I felt strongly drawn to her. I just couldn't pin exactly why—and no, it's not because of the things I just told you.

"Hey, hun, I have to get to that teachers' meeting I was telling you about. Can you keep an eye on things while I'm gone?" she asks Valery, but her eyes were looking at me; *she's asking her daughter to babysit me. This is great*, I think unenthusiastically.

"Yeah sure, Mom, see you later," she replies with a knowing smile. *Great, she even knows it too!* I accidentally let out a groan, but in my state, they didn't pay much attention. After giving the keys to Valery, she leaves the class and shuts the door.

"So you going to explain how you got this beat up?" she asks, putting a gentle hand on my shoulder. I don't know how or why. But the minute she does, I feel like I'm on a sugar rush, like I couldn't feel pain in a single skin cell. With her rubbing my shoulder gently, I begin telling her how I got on the bad side of Chase Maxwell and how the rest followed.

"That is so low," she comments at the end.

"Yeah, I know," I say, remembering all the crap he's made me do.

"Like really, how mean can someone be!" she basically shouts, throwing her arms in the air. Just then, all my pain cascades on me once again, making me see spots.

"Yeah," I grunt in agreement.

"So what are you going to do?" she asks simply.

"What do you mean?" I ask afraid of her answer.

"Well, aren't you going to get him back?" she asks, putting a hand on my forearm. I felt great. *I could get him back*, I think feeling a smile creeping on my face. *He deserves it too!*

"Yeah…I will…and I know how too," I say with an evil smile pasted on my face as I tell her my idea.

"That's crazy! If he finds out that was you, there might not be enough left of you to heal," she says with a concerned look on her face as she looks up from wrapping some of my minor injuries.

"But it's foolproof!" I say. "All I have to do is switch the playing ball with one with a magnetic center, put some metal on his bat, some metal on his bat so that the two objects will repel with such force that he doesn't even have to hit the ball to get a home run. Chase is good, but everyone will know that something is wrong, and he'll be kicked off the team for cheating!" I say exuding confidence, maybe for the first time in my life.

"But how are you going to get away?" she asks. *Ugh! Why didn't I think of that?* I give a shudder but hide it with a thoughtful look.

"Before the game when they're all practicing, I'll do it, then I'll hide under the bleachers till the games over," I say sensibly.

"Okay…but being under there all night? Maybe I could pick you up," she says; she looked deep in thought, which made it even harder to burst her bubble.

"Um…Valery, not to be rude, but can you even drive?" I ask in my nicest innocent voice, trying to mimic my sister.

"Well...not exactly, but I have a friend that can drive us," she says. I had a vague feeling it was her mom, but I let it slide.

"Sure, okay, where and when do you want to meet?" I ask.

"Umm, well, we can meet under the bleachers. I'll bring this light so you know it's me," she says, holding up a red-colored flashlight.

"Yeah, okay, cool. So what about the time?" I ask simply.

"How 'bout like maybe ten to fifteen minutes after the game starts? By then Chase will be up to bat, which will give us the perfect diversion" she asks with a "*sound good?*" look.

"Yeah, sounds good," I reply, managing to sit up with her help. "Okay, but now I have to put a magnet in every baseball that the school owns, so I'll only have to focus on the bat when the games about to start," starting for the door; she meets me there.

"Okay...just be careful, will you?" she asks hesitantly. I smile genuinely through the bruises.

"Of course, I don't know about you, but I'm kind of tired of getting beat up," I say still smiling. That earns me a giggle as she slides her hand from my upper arm to my hand, and squeezes it supportively. I mouth a *thanks*, and I walk out trying to ignore the pain everywhere, and trying to focus on the electric feeling still in my hand.

While I was in Mrs. Jackson's class, Valery managed to wrap my right arm in an ace bandage and put Neosporin on the cuts and scrapes on my face and my other arm. The bruises still ached, and the pain in my face wasn't gone for long since Tylenol and Ibuprofen were out of the question. But even without it, I felt stronger than before; Valery is a miracle worker.

I skip the rest of school to plant remote-controlled magnetic chips in all of the baseballs, so no matter what, my plan would work—and my parents said robotics club was a waste of time.

I decide to stay and catch up on some reading while I wait till the game, and the longer I waited the more anxious I became. Finally when it was time to put the other chip on the bat, I executed it with military precision, keeping my hood on I make my way to the bleachers hoping no one was paying attention to me. I sneak under the bleachers already regretting my hiding spot, but I had to wait for Valery. That's when I bump into the one and only Chelsey O'Neil. After her screaming and some conversation, I was getting really anxious, she could give away my hiding spot. So I cover her mouth, only for her to bite me. Gee, this is turning out t be a wonderful day! (cough, cough, sarcasm, cough!)

"OW," I exclaim angrily, and that's when everything goes downhill. Not too long after I start talking to Chelsey, I see the familiar red light, but there was two. *Well, I have been suffering from double vision as of late*, I reassure myself. But when Chelsey lets out a scream, I know that something is seriously wrong.

I feel something on my arm and turn to see the one person I feared more than anyone in the whole freaking world, Chase Maxwell…with red eyes? Unexpectedly

Chase puts a cloth over my face; since when did he worry about people hearing us? The cloth has a very sweet, almost too sweet smell... *maybe it's not for my screaming...?* But before I can do anything, I'm out like a light.

VALERY JACKSON

"Valery, I need you to open up the classroom for Josh. He's the one who comes and cleans all the class equipment. He knows what to do, but I am going to be in meetings all day, so I can't open up today, but I will be there for lunch okay?" says my mom from the counter in the teachers' lounge. She was pouring herself some coffee while I was sipping on my green tea with milk and sugar.

"Yeah, okay, no problem," I say a bit anxiously, the way my mom talks about him. I wouldn't be surprised if he were the president of the United States. I don't know why I was so anxious. I guess I just wanted someone like me, someone smart, someone who understands what being picked on feels like, someone that is a friend.

"Okay, well, he should be here any minute, have fun!" she says in that way of hers that I could never duplicate. My mom is really probably the best teacher in this school. I'm an only child, but she makes it seem like all her students are her children too. Like I guess what I'm trying to say is that she understands them better than other teachers do.

"Okay, bye!" I say happily sipping on my tea as she leaves the room. I finish my tea then go to the mirror in the bathroom to make sure my sandy-brown hair hasn't gone completely frizzy; it gets really humid in Florida. Other than my hair, I have brown eyes and a tanned round face. I'm average height, and the only thing that isn't average about me is my IQ.

I get to my mom's science class and open it up and turn on the lights. I sit on a desk and leisurely read the wall art. What feels like hours must only be minutes, but when the sub walks in and starts shuffling through papers, I get a tad worried; I look at my watch, which reads *7:05 a.m.*

"I'm going to be late!" I say to no one in particular and rush out of the class, bidding a hasty farewell to Mrs. Barmy and scurry to my first period class, making it to my seat the second the bell rings. I let out a breath that I hadn't realized I was holding and get to work on the algebra problems on the board—easy, easy, easy. I'm still a freshman, but Monday I will be a sophomore so I can participate in a harder curriculum.

The first half of the day passed fairly quickly, almost in a blur, and the next thing I know is I'm eating lunch with my mom when someone from outside knocks quietly on the door to the classroom. I get up from eating my sandwich and open the door to a tall beat-up boy; his lips are forming words but nothing comes out, then he falls into my arms unconscious.

"Mom, help!" I yell, but she was already by my side.

"Josh! Are you all right?" she yells.

"Wait…This is Josh?" I ask surprised. My mom nods her head gravely.

Josh was not what I had expected. My mom said he got picked on too, but I didn't realize he got beaten. Under all the cuts and bruises, he looked like a possibly strange kid; he was extremely tall with slick black hair that curled towards the bottom. He's so beat up I couldn't tell if that was how his nose originally looked or if it were crushed to smithereens when he was getting beat up.

Meanwhile, she and I push some tables together and lay him on top, kind of like an operating table. He really looked dead; I lay my hand on his hand while my mom continues to yell.

"Josh, Josh! Are you okay?" Jeez, he's beat up, not deaf.

"Um, well, I feel like I'm dead. Does that count as okay?" he asks sarcastically.

"Well, you're obviously well enough for sarcasm, I say you'll live. What about you, Valery?" says my mom, giving Josh a smile.

"Yeah, he'll live," I say, really impressed that he can still manage sarcasm.

"Oh, I don't believe we've met. I'm Josh Williams," he says, trying to get up for me to shake his hand, but I stop him.

"Slowly!" I say and urgently pushing him back down. As I touch him, it feels like I stuck my finger in a light socket, but at the same time, it felt oddly nice.

"Thanks," he says through clenched teeth.

"No problem," I start. "My name is Valery Jackson."

"Wait, did you say—"

"Yeah, I'm Samantha Jackson's daughter," I interrupt.

"Wait…so you're Mrs. Jackson's daughter?" he asks, mystified. "So do you go to this school? I…I…um, don't remember seeing you before," he continues to talk. "What grade?"

"Yeah, I go here, and this week my teachers decided it would be best for me to skip a grade, so it can be more challenging for me and all...so I'm in your grade starting Monday," I say, feeling a bit self-conscious

"Hey, hun, I have to get to that teachers' meeting I was telling you about. Can you keep an eye on things while I'm gone?" asks my mom.

"Yeah sure, Mom, see you later," I say, happy she's leaving us alone; then after a couple of minutes, she leaves the room.

"So you want to explain how you got this beat up?" I state, not even realizing I was touching his shoulder; and again, it feels like I got electrocuted, in a good way. Does that make sense? Oh god, I'm going crazy. Meanwhile, he talks about what happened, I feel so, so disturbed at what a little thing he did to deserve something like that. *We have to get revenge!* I think.

"So what are you going to do?" I ask plaintively.

"What do you mean?" he asks.

"Well, aren't you going to get him back?" I ask, and that's how we finally get somewhere.

The next thing I know, Josh is running out to put magnets on all the baseballs in the school so he can get Chase kicked off the team for cheating; it was brilliant actually, and I almost feel jealous that I hadn't thought of that.

Before he left, I couldn't help myself, I squeeze his hand. The second I do, I feel my fingers tingle with electricity, and my whole body is buzzing with the familiar energy; but it felt different this time, less shocking and more of that other feeling, like the aftertaste of really good ice cream. I release his hand, and he's on his way; and for another minute or so, the feeling continues up my arms and up my spine, making me shudder in delight.

Now I just had to wait…and wait, monotonously for hours, still trying to hold on to that tingly feeling.

When the time came for me to leave, Sandra was already ringing the doorbell. Sandra's one of my mom's students that has always struck me as a smooth, even-toned person, that and she can drive. So we're off. I go over the plan with her as we go, and I feel that this plan will go perfect. Well, I thought that before I got there anyway.

We arrive right when I say I would, so I run full sprint to the bleachers, but I'm stopped short as I see Chase Maxwell carrying a limp Josh. *He is going to die!* is my last sane thought—well, semisane thought—before I charge into Chase full tackle, but I basically bounce off him as if he were made of metal; he doesn't even seem struck by it. *What gives?* I think, confused and angry.

"Let him go you insane jerk!" I shriek at the top of my lungs, but he doesn't reply and neither does anyone else. *Why is everyone just watching?* I think, mystified and feeling defeated already.

But I wasn't about to lose a friend. *This is what friends do…right?* I think, trying to build my nerve, but that only cascaded doubts on me like, *Were we even friends? Chase is too strong, wouldn't friends want the other friend to be safe too even though something bad might happen to them? What if he kills us both? What if he only kills one of us? What if he makes life a living hell till we're basically pleading to die? Why am I so afraid of Chase?* But that last one actually helped for what it's worth, like seriously; I was basically calling him a murderer, and he was a sophomore. He is sure a bully, but he wouldn't kill…would he?

Well, I felt really big just then, enough to stand a little taller and scream.

"You are a jerk. The only reason you pick on Josh is because you are threatened by how amazingly smart he is…and now you're done, you're done bullying him, bullying anyone and everyone, and I promise you I will make sure of it!" I say boldly, strongly determined. That of course is when he jumps five feet in the air with Josh still over his shoulder.

He lands on me with a sickening thud. Everything was blurry for a minute, then something was put over my mouth, and before I could protest, before I could even feel my own breathing, I was dead. Well, not dead, dead. But I wasn't conscious either.

LILIA RIDER

I can be a touchy person. Scratch that, actually, if you touch me, you'll lose your fingers, period. And if that doesn't scare you off, then your name must be Adam Shards—you'll see why later.

I'm average height; Adam is a little taller. I have blond hair with brown low lights; Adam has light golden-brown hair. I have angular features making me look almost…sharp. Adam has rounded features, making him look constantly happy. I have thin lips and a small pointed nose while Adam has full lips with a medium-sized nose that's rounded too. I have nearly pale skin while Adam is tanned.

I can hardly stand people in general; they're all way too loud and annoying. But I really can't stand him; it's not like he knows me. I'm invisible to pretty much everyone. Adam is what you might call a big-headed jock. But I don't care how many people swarm around him, I wouldn't want to hang out with any of those stupid jocks or girly girls anyway, but he just seems so stuck up like no one's worth his attention unless they are in high places too.

In my opinion, he dresses a bit trashy. He's always wearing sweatshirts with basketball shorts that go low enough to see his boxers. That, and you can't forget the hat; I don't think I've ever seen him without it. It's a blue flat bill that covers almost all of his hair, except for the long strands that curl around it.

While I, Lilia Rider, dress in my typical attire of dark skinny jeans with an equally dark T-shirt with my hair brushed out straight. And to top it all off, my favorite yellow sneakers.

We, in a sense, are mere opposites.

The school day was halfway over; I was sitting alone in my typical spot by the basketball court to avoid this one bully named Mark—but I'll get to that later. I'm pretty predictable. I even bring two lunches—like I said, I'll get to that later. And I eat the same thing every day: a peanut butter and jelly sandwich cut diagonally, apple slices, and water, plain maybe, but last time I checked, I didn't ask your opinion.

Down below there were the regular boys shooting three pointers. But they seemed unusually quiet; the basketball court was almost silent except for the squeak of shoes and the dribble of the basketball.

Why was it so quite? That's when I noticed; Mark's here. *Could he be here for me?* I think to myself in a panic. Then as I'm looking for an escape route, out of thin air, there sitting in front of me is, of course, Adam Shards. I pretend not to notice him looking at me, and of course, what does he do? With his stupid swagger says, "Hey, what's up?"

This only made me mad, one, because he was going to draw attention to me, and two, he doesn't even know me. Why talk to me now? I look at the basketball court where Mark's dribbling the ball.

"The sky," I say tightly and go back to my sandwich. He lets out a chuckle. *Urg! Go away!*

"So…," he starts. *Why was he here anyway?*

"Why are you talking to me?" I ask with a sheer bitterness to my voice, but he didn't catch my anger or chose to ignore it.

"Well, I saw you sitting up here alone and wanted to know if you wanted to learn how to play basketball," he says with almost heartbreaking kindness that really pissed me off.

"Why?" I bite out.

"Because it would be fun…and if you haven't noticed already, too many people are gone to play a good game," he replies smoothly.

"No," I say plainly and turn my full attention to my sandwich. *If I go down there, it will be like suicide*, I think, swallowing a lump in my throat.

"Oh come on, you could use a little fun," he says with a persuasive tone. Why was he being so nice to me? I was just too curious, and without thinking, I say, "Why are you being so nice to me? Is this some kind of bet?"

This catches him off guard, but only for a second before he replies.

"I don't know, I guess I'm in a good mood. And no, this isn't a bet," he says with reasonable logic, yet this still unchanged my mood.

"Whatever," I reply. He smiles wickedly.

"Come on," he says with a smile and then tries to pull me out of my seat playfully. He was strong even for a playful tug; he is tall and bulky, but he is slow. So I use that to my advantage.

He continues to pull me, and I let him for about two more seconds planning my strategy.

"Cut it out," I growl, knowing if he went and tattled on me I needed some sort of defense, but he persisted. "Look, hurting you is not on my agenda, but I can make an exception," I say, readying my stance.

"I doubt you could hurt me. Come on, it would be fu—"

But before he could finish his sentence, I stiff leg him, going for the surprise attack. And just like that, he's on his knees. He tries to get up, but I wasn't finished; hey, he insulted me, so it's only right to make a point here and there. With one hand, I push him on his stomach; my other hand was twisting his arm around his back in a police hold.

He was as vulnerable as a baby, always was really. Just a slight flick of my wrist could give a truckload of pain; a more obvious twist could break something. Adam winces but he keeps whatever pain I'm giving him inside. *Not bad, Shards*, I think, slightly impressed. *But you're still on the ground*, I think with a smile. For some reason, I just didn't have it in me. Gripping his shoulder with my viselike grip, I start to relax.

"Don't...touch...me," I say through gritted teeth. I wanted to add "*next time it will be worse*," but I had a feeling there wouldn't be a next time. Satisfied, I drop my hand to my side and stand up, grab my lunch, and scale the bleachers till I find a new spot that suites me.

"So is that a yes?" he asks sarcasm in his voice even though I probably embarrassed him in front of his basketball buddies; he still had that stupid smile on his face.

"You just don't know when to let go, don't you!" I exclaim. Hey, who could blame me? I was seeing red. Trying to compose myself, I return my full attention once again to my lunch, stick my earbuds in, and turn the volume up. I sneak a peek at Mark who's still shooting three pointers. I don't check if Adam leaves, but he hasn't bugged me again, so I assume he went with his basketball buds.

I was wrong yet again.

I have five minutes before lunch ends; I finish up my food and make my way to the trash bin at the bottom of the bleachers. But when I get up, it seems like out of nowhere Adam Shards is there with a tray that had his leftovers on it—and by what was on his tray, he must love greasy cheeseburgers with lots of ketchup and mustard.

He seemed as surprised as I was but still the scene went down like this. He *accidentally trips* into me, his tray falls so he can hold his hand out to catch himself, the tray spills everywhere, including on me. And lastly, he pushes me down with him; I hit my head on the stair with a thud, instantly getting a splintering migraine.

For a second, I feel as though I can't breathe. Then I look not even inches away from my face, lying on top of me like the big oaf he is, is Adam Shards. And for the septillionth time today, I'm reminded in flying colors why I hate him.

"Oh jeez, I am so sorry!" he says while getting off me. He holds out his hand to help me up, but I scowl at him and get up by myself. When I'm up, I reach out to try and grab him by the collar of his shirt, but as I try to reach him, a wave of nausea hits me, and I stagger back to the ground.

"ADAM!" I say, anger taking hold of me. "What, is this all because I refused to play basketball?" I yell, but I wasn't looking for an answer. I regain some of my balance; my composer on the other hand was gone.

"No! I swear I was over by the trashcans, I was going to throw my stuff away, then I'm here. No joke, I would never do this on purpose! Why would you think that?" he says with a confused, concerned, and slightly irritated expression on his face.

"Oh, I don't know! Maybe because you were like, '*Oh come on, Lilia! You could use a little fun*!'" I say, my voice sliding into his deeper more gravelly voice with ease, no big deal—to me. But to Adam Shards…He looked like he either wanted to pass out or hit me with a shovel.

"How…How did you do…do that?" he asks shakily. *Guess it's option A: pass out.*

"Do what?" I asked innocently although I was definitely freaking out in my head.

"How did you make your voice sound exactly like mine!" he says with fear in his pathetic voice.

"Oh please, besides you have a very girly voice. It's easy to imitate. Think of that?" I remark. In truth, I don't even know where it came from, yet it felt so easy. *Could I do that before?*

"No, I know what I heard…that was exactly my voice," he said with furrowed brows.

"Wow, I'm the one who hit my head, and you're the one hallucinating? I think you should get to the nurse," I say casually, and to really get under his skin, I hold my head again close my eyes like I'm in pain and let out a little groan; he frowns, clearly upset, and drops the subject obviously not happy, and he was off my back. *Bonus!*

"Anyway…I'm sorry I spilled on you," he said a bit softer. That's when I realize that I still have ketchup and mustard spilled everywhere. I reach for a napkin from his tray and get to work. But in the end, it was no use. I had ketchup *everywhere. It looks like an FBI crime scene.*

"Excuse me while I head to the nurse, maybe she will have a change of clothes," I say grumpily completely forgetting Mark.

"Um, okay…Hey, do you think I can make this up to you?" he asks with a mixture of concern and hope; I just wanted to get out of there.

"No," I say.

"Please?"

"NO!"

"PLEASE!"

"NO!!!"

"PLEASE!!!" he said so loudly the whole gym goes silent.

"Fine, whatever, just leave me alone!" I say quietly in his ear as I'm walking down. Feeling everyone's eyes on me—especially Mark's—I try to keep my head low. That, and I feel so frustrated and exhausted I just want to get out of here. *Alone.*

He sighs. "Cool, I'll get back to you on that," he says with a mischievous smile.

"Whatever," I say, trying not to notice it, and walk off the bleachers and out of the gym

I head straight for the nurse; I try my best not to walk funny, but eventually, it became unbearable. By the time I reached the front office, I was waddling like a penguin. It was so embarrassing. *I'm going to get him for this!* I promise to myself.

"Oh dear!" says the front office lady named Carrie; she had a bit of a Southern drawl and beach-blond hair. She wore plaid shirts and cowboy boots every day, and she was definitely better than my stupid ole teachers. "What happened to you? Please tell me Mark didn't do this to you!" she said with a horrified look on her face.

I told you I would get back to him…unfortunately.

Mark was a boy who had bullied me since the second grade; he's been suspended more times than I can count, but since his parents are big supporters of the school and the head of the school board, he's here to stay. But that wasn't the point. Lately his bullying has…spiraled out of control; like now, I'm bringing two lunches and I'm eating on the bleachers where he won't go.

And it's not that I couldn't beat the kid into the ground, it's that he could snap his fingers and all of a sudden I am in Mesopotamia studying camel poop. Did I mention he's a spoiled rich kid that can do practically whatever he wants? Like the president of the United States is bowing at his feet. Man, I would give anything to break those stubby little fingers of his.

"No, this is the work of a klutz," I say, unsticking my head from the clouds.

"Here you go," says Carrie, handing me some spare clothes from the community bin, most stuff was donation only, and it needed some serious cleaning. What she handed me was a pair of old basketball shorts and a red T-shirt with some basketball logo on it, but it wasn't covered in ketchup and is the cleanest shirt in the pile. Ugh!

I quickly rush to the little girl's room and try to wash off the ketchup as best I can. I get dressed in a rush. And when I finally look in the mirror, I almost didn't recognize myself. My hair is gnarled; there are streaks of ketchup and mustard everywhere. And over all, I was a mess—I'm not very self-conscious about my outfits and hairstyle, so that's saying a lot.

I get to work on my hair; at first, I try to use my fingers, but I stopped when large clumps of hair got caught around my fingers and fell to the ground in front of me. Then I tried wetting it in the sink in the bathroom. At least it got some of the gnarls out. But now my hair is wet as a dog's and dripping everywhere, and no there was no towel; I was not happy.

I am forced to go to my next class, so I say bye to Carrie, the coolest person ever, and make my way to Mr. Grature's class, fourth period. When I finally get there, Mr. Grature is teaching the class about the Punic wars. I walk in slowly then make a quick dash to my seat; I bow my head on my desk and hope no one is looking my way; they weren't of course. No one does.

The class period was almost over, and I was officially zoning out when the intercom crackled to life; all I heard was my name and office—*What?* Everyone looks at me expectantly; Mr. Grature nodded my way. Oh! I was called down to the office, *but I was just down there.*

I look around once more, then I realize…Adam isn't here! For some reason, I had a creeping suspicion that whatever I was going down to the office for had something to do with Adam Shards. And so my curiosity taking over, I get out of my seat and walk out of the classroom. If only someone had warned me that the expression curiosity killed the cat was more than just a cute saying.

I'm walking down the hall when my worst nightmare literally runs right into me; I stumble backwards just from the shock of him being there. He looked sort of different, less groomed.

He normally wears a nice pair of perfectly creased slacks, a button-up shirt with either brown or black leather shoes. His sleeves are always at his wrists, and there's never as much as a wrinkle on his whole attire. His blond hair is always combed back, and he always wears that smug expression; he looks like a young business tycoon.

But now, his sleeves are rolled up to his elbows; his hair is parted a little to the left of his face, and it's curlier. His pants are regular jeans, and when I get a better look at his shirt, the pattern is actually dirt. A worried look crowds out the smugness on his face, and his dark gray eyes look like a gruesome thundercloud. Something was definitely wrong here.

"Let's go, princess," he says gruffly and grabs my arm with a lot more strength than I've ever seen him use. Had he had this before, or is this a new side effect from the new wardrobe?

"Why?" I ask annoyed. That's when he pulls out a gun, holy—

"I said let's go!" he shouts like a psycho.

"Okay, okay, let's not do anything rash here," I say calmly. "Why are you doing this, Mark?" I ask, trying to hide my fear; his eyes turn a milky shade of gray, and his whole demeanor changes from anxious to mock horror psycho.

"He'll kill me, he killed everyone, just like his other relatives, we're all going to die!" he rambles incoherently, and in truth, I was about to wet myself.

"Slow down, who's going to kill you? And who else did he kill?" I ask, feeling my heart in my ears.

"He—he…he kills everyone. We're all going to die," he continues.

"Okay, Mark, just take me where you were going to before," I say as calmly as I can.

"Hole!" he shouts.

"Mark, what hole?" I ask, looking down to see perfectly carpeted hole-free ground. "Mark, listen to me, put away the gun and sit down," I say, looking him in the eyes; for a second, he seems to recall where he is and calms down. His fingers are no longer on the trigger. Good, a fast roundhouse will knock it out of his hand. By the time he realizes he doesn't have his gun, I will do a back kick to knock him off balance, then I will punch him in the solar plexus and then I'm home free.

"Lilia!" comes the familiar voice. *Damn it!*

But fortunately, Mark turns, giving me a window. I kick the gun right out of his hands; it lands on the ground and skids farther away. Shocked Mark starts to turn around, but by the time he's facing me, he's got a foot to the chest. Now in most cases that type of kick would only faze an opponent, but since Mark wasn't ready, he lost balance and fell to the ground.

"Lilia, are you okay?" asks Adam.

"Let's see, I almost got shot by possibly the worst person alive, and you almost got us killed!" I say angrily.

"Oh my god, I'm so sorry. I didn't mean to—"

"Save it!" I shout frustrated; he looks hurt, but at the moment, I don't really care. From here on, everything went downhill, fast.

ADAM SHARDS

Well, Lilia sure set the scene. Now unlike what she might say, I was going a little wacko at the time. Normally I do not spill my lunch on people—no joke, I seriously wasn't even near here, then *poof*! I'm literally falling over her! This is such a weird day... like when do you get accused of intentionally trying to get people killed because we have some psychos at our school who bring guns to school and somehow control gravity! Oh, Lilia didn't explain? Wow, this is going really bad already, wonderful! Let me just start from the beginning. To those of you rolling your eyes, quit it!

So anyways, what do you get a girl that hates your guts? The whole rest of the day I had been trying to think of what I could do to make it up to her, then I stumble on another wrinkle: I don't even know what she likes—I know, for liking her so much I sure don't know much about her—so maybe some flowers? No, super cheesy…maybe jewelry? No, even worse…I could do her homework? No! I could get her in trouble…I know! I could get that bully off her back! She would like that right? Don't you just love my thinking process?

Okay, so I got the why, what, and who...Now I just need the where, how, and when.

Okay, let's think of where and when, obviously it doesn't have to be today, but surprise would be on my side—and from Lilia's demonstration on the bleachers, surprise shouldn't be underestimated. Now Mark isn't the most discreet person; he will probably be in the courtyard blackmailing some innocent kid into doing his homework, so I'll make an excuse to leave class and hopefully I can end his reign for good.

I feel pretty good right now, knowing that not only will I help Lilia, but almost everyone in this school who's ever crossed Mr. Weasel himself. So I let my ego get ahead of me, I make an excuse to leave class, just to find him, you know, a little surveillance couldn't hurt.

Now, in my mind, I knew the only way we could ever get Mark out of this school is for him to leave voluntarily, so maybe give him something to be scared of for once, show him that I'm not scared by his pathetic blackmail.

But the fight ends before it begins

I see Mark, he looks...different. Do I care? Nope, I just continue watching. I see him with Lilia; not knowing the context, I just assumed that he was trying to show off or something like that, then when I see the look on his face, let's just say it'll give me nightmares. I don't even see the gun before it's too late. Thank heavens Lilia is pro at stuff like this, or we would be in some serious trouble...kind of like how I am right now for nearly getting both of us killed. It didn't really matter though, Mark looked down for the count; he wasn't exactly what a person would call fit anyway. I wouldn't be surprised if he's knocked out for a couple of minutes. And besides, by then we'll have it all under control. It's just kind of weird…like normally he's so precise, almost robotic. To have a mental breakdown would be the last thing a fortune-teller would foresee in his future. So what gives?

But of course, I think of these things one turn too late; as a result, almost inhumanly, Mark literally flies up from the ground and floats a foot off the ground. Okay, so when you see someone doing that, at first you might be in awe. Not me. No, he rose up like an evil villain on their last stand, completely crazed. I would've run too if it weren't for me being literally glued to the ground. It was like the little weasel had control over gravity too.

Whatever's in his head is something that I don't want to know, but I had that feeling that I was going to find out anyway. I look over at Lilia who seems to be dealing with the same problem.

"Lilia and Adam, you have been chosen, you may except or face the consequences," says Mark in a voice definitely not his.

"And what have we been 'chosen for' exactly?" asks Lilia, still sounding like her usually annoyed self. But he only repeats himself in that creepy voice of his.

"And what if I decline? What are you going to do, turn me into a frog?" she asks mockingly. *Why a frog?* I can't help but wonder. But my question sadly won't be answered because as she says this, his face turns from red to purple to white. Then, his eyes…glow, and in a swift motion, his hand rises and so does Lilia—well, I was right on the gravity part I guess— his arm moves with force, back and forth, back and forth. Along dragging a defenseless Lilia at the mercy of a psycho.

"Stop, you're hurting her!" I shout, finally finding my voice. He drops Lilia in a heap on the ground and turns to me.

"Your decision," he says flatly in that weird voice.

"I don't care, just don't hurt her!" I say breathlessly. Mark turns back towards Lilia, almost like he's sizing her up for slaughter.

"Your decision," he says louder, looking at me again.

"Sure, fine, I accept," I say, looking at Lilia; she was barely alive, but I could almost feel her disappointment. Then Mark does something that nearly killed me. He took a knife out of his hand. Like not out of his jacket, it was like out of his hand, like an improved version of Wolverine in X-men, and moves to cut her. I look away knowing what's in front of me. This is definitely the worst day ever. But then, unexpectedly, I hear a voice.

"Adam?"

She was alive! I turn to see her holding her throat as if she were choking, which she wasn't, for then she says with bitter sweetness.

"Watch out! He's got something in his—"

And with that, everything went black. Like I said, she was alive, yet well I'm not sure about myself at this point. I can't feel anything, but the weight of my thoughts. Only a strange sort of blackness, it's hard to explain; but Mark did use something, it must've been chloroform, but what was that smell…bleach? No, it couldn't. But whatever it was, it was strong; only a few people have access to things this strong. What is happening?

Of course, I didn't have to ponder that question for long because after what feels like five minutes of darkness, a stark white, incredibly bright light turns on.

"OW," I say, wincing from the burning light. *Am I in heaven?* I think stupidly. Hey, give me a break. I have had the weirdest day today. That's when I hear it again…the voice, her voice!

"Lilia?" I say, still blinded from the lights.

"Adam?" she says in response. "Where are we? What happened?" she asks, voicing the question that I hadn't even had time to think of.

"I don't know," I say lamely.

My eyes were still adjusting—having spots in my eyes probably isn't a good sign, huh?— Well, that's when I take the time to look around, and to be honest, I would've fallen over in my chair if I weren't chained to it! Looking around, there was about twelve chairs all arranged in a little semicircle. But the worst part was, is that we weren't the only ones.

BAY TINE

April 5. School's almost over, the sun a little brighter, and of course the homework just the same. But I don't care; it feels as though my whole life is wrapped around school, from its wide hallways to its noisy cafeteria to its huge classrooms. I find myself trying to beg the clock to go slower, unsuccessfully of course. Still, it's not that I don't like any other place either; it's just that school seems like a place where I can always belong, where all the worries of the outside world blur together, and almost disappear. Pushed into a place so deep in my mind that it's almost lost entirely.

As I walk down the wide halls, I sense a tall, quiet figure behind me—Andrew. He's tall with dark brown hair and dark coffee eyes that seem to cut through me into my thoughts. He always wore dark clothes—probably so it wouldn't draw attention away from his face. I want to be around him all the time, but whenever I do, it's like my tongue gets away from myself; and I'm either talking about the weather or some really stupid story. But it doesn't matter; just being around him feels like a calming breeze.

I guess I picture him a bit too perfect; of course, he has his merits, but when I can, I look right past them. I like the way he smiles, even his cheesy fake smile that he uses on some of my pathetic jokes. I like his personality, his laugh, and when they're all stacked up on one another, it's like he's turned into someone capable of being perfect.

I, on the other hand, have blond hair, am sort of tall—for a girl, at least. I also love wearing funny T-shirts: anything colorful really. You know, for the fun of it. Like most teens, I have some acne—which bugs me so freaking much. But hey! Nothing proactive can't fix... hopefully.... But to finish, I have large brown eyes, a small nose, and a normal sized mouth.

"Hey, Andrew, what's up?" I ask.

"Nothing much," he replies tiredly. *Hmm...should I ask him why he's tired, or go straight into the part where there's a sky and a sun that's up...*

"You seem...worn out. Something wrong?" I ask sincerely. He lets out a tired sigh.

"I don't know, just tired. I've been working on this thing—"

"What thing?" I ask, interrupting him.

"Oh, this little book report that's due tomorrow... and well, I'm still on chapter ten in the book," he says cautiously. *Oh boy.*

"What's it on?" I ask, worried this conversation has gone south.

"On this book called *The True Confessions of Charlotte Doyle.*"

"Ooh! I've read that. It's really good. It's like a combination of historical fiction, mystery, and adventure!" I say, remembering the story like I had read it yesterday.

"Yeah, it's okay, but it's kind of *girly*," he says with an emphases on girly.

"Well, how would you know? You've only read till chapter ten!" I say, my voice rising in agitation. I try to laugh it off but it was hollow, and he obviously looked hurt.

"Hey, I didn't mean girly, girly. I meant like right now there's not enough action going on," he said, realizing his mistake. I relaxed a bit.

"Hey, it's historical fiction. There's not going to be suicide bombers dropping nukes on their heads," I say, laughing in my high soft voice that I had been aiming for earlier.

"Well, I get that, but I just wish there is some more action that's all," he insisted.

"Sure, but not all adventure is good," I say with a sigh. "Next thing you know, you'll be kidnapped by some lunatic," I say teasingly.

"Yeah right, this is like the safest neighborhood in Idaho... and besides, I just meant the book really—," he starts. "But I must admit, classes are getting kind of boring." I almost wanted to clap just then.

"Anyway...what are you going to do?" I ask, bringing back the old topic. Just then I felt like clapping myself, in the head.

"I don't know, get the book summary from the Internet and base it off that," he says with a tired sigh.

I felt bad, but what could I do? I couldn't do it for him, and helping is like too many people at a plate...so what could I do? I was stuck, but before I could reply, the bell rang; and we made our hasty good-byes as we hustled to our next class.

Before I knew it, third period came and went; unfortunately, so did lunch, goodness! I blew another chance to talk to Andrew! I thought with a scowl, still the memory of Andrew was still repeating in my mind. *If only you knew just how much I liked you!* I think bitterly to myself, wishing Andrew could somehow hear my thoughts from two classrooms down. Okay, so from what you have just read, you're probably shaking your head right now, but believe me, that was a low point in our conversations. Outside of school, we could talk for hours and then some.

As fourth period eased by, I decided to drop the topic and listen to the lesson; today felt unusual, like when do I ever drift off in class? When do I get to school less than five minutes early? Why were we having so many subs? That last one was a stupid question. The teachers were at some convention about this new leadership program; it sounded interesting but not enough to wrap my mind around, yet I still had the weird prickly feeling at the back of my mind, nagging at me, trying to get me to listen, but to what?

Fifth period comes in and replaces fourth and still the nagging feeling only felt stronger, like it was coming soon; why can't it just be written out for me! No, it's never written to you or told to you in anything other than a stinking riddle or some unsolvable puzzle that has no picture, not even the box for help. *How come the secrets of the universe cant just present themselves?* Yep, I'm going crazy. Like what the heck? Secrets of the universe, where did that come from? But to my amazement, the intercom cackles to life. Could this be for me?

"Sorry for the interruption, Bay Tine is to report to the office immediately, that will be all," said the monotone voice; I wasn't sure if I should be nervous or exited.

The next thing that I can remember was that I was approaching the office window, that's when I see them. No, could they be for me? They couldn't! I haven't done anything wrong! Then they must be for someone else, maybe we're going to have a fire drill! I thought with not so much as a dent in my doubt.

Cautiously, I walk in. The officers turn toward me, and in unison, they asked,

"Are you Miss Bay Tine?" I was too in a daze to reply, just vaguely I remember myself nodding, then as if robotic they both bid me to follow them. What was this all for? Before I could even make a guess, one of the police officers offer me a seat in the chair next to the principal's desk; I obey wordlessly.

"Miss Tine—"

"Please call me Bay," I say quietly but interrupting him the same.

"Bay, your mother and father both work as pharmacists, is that correct?" he began.

"Yes," I replied hoarsely.

"And they normally take the freeway...together to go to work, am I still correct?" This time I could only nod, that little scratch at the back of my mind feeling more like a cat toying with a mouse. But the mouse was my insides.

"Well, if that is all true, we believe that your mother and father were the two people in the crash this afternoon. I'm so very sorry to have to tell you this, but we believe that your parents were hit by a moving truck whose doors were not secured correctly. The truck stopped, and the contents hit their car. They were pronounced dead at the scene," he said in the calmest voice. I hated that voice. *Was this all a joke, a prank some sick person thinks would be amusing? Well, it's not funny!* Sure I knew he felt bad, not as bad as me though.

Then as he continued to talk, he began to lay out some objects; they seemed tattered and scratched, but I would recognize them anywhere. He placed the small necklace that I had made in the first grade on the desk. It spelled out "OUR FAMILY UNITED" in aqua and pink glitter beads; the thread was just about to snap, and some of the letters had been scratched out; so now it said " UR I T ". The rest were faded so badly the colors seemed to turn white before my eyes.

Along with the necklace, he laid out a thin cloth; it was black, but now it was frayed on the sides and had fading spots—my dad's jacket! I couldn't believe it. I didn't trust myself to speak. Thankfully, the officer saw my distress. "These were found at the sight. You may keep them if you would like, but the rest must be evidence, I am truly sorry for your loss," he says in a soft, respectful voice. "Now I am supposed to take you to your grandmother's. She will meet us at the station downtown," he continued. I could only nod my head, too stunned. I couldn't believe that it had only been a few minutes. *So that's it? No one last good-bye?*

I remembered the last time I had talked to them.

"Bye, Mom. Bye, Dad!" I yelled up the stairs. "I'm heading out to the bus stop!" I say with every intention of walking, but just like every day, Mom appears at the top of the stairs, her hair in a loose bun with a curly tendril of blond hair framing her left cheek; she smiles and runs down the stairs to meet me.

"Hi, honey, just give me a sec, and your dad and I can drive you," she said, her smile not fading; it was always hard to resist Mom. So I didn't—now that I think about it, it's the best decision I've ever made.

"Okay, but I have to leave real soon," I warned; she knows I hate being late.

"Don't worry, honey, just hop in the car, and we will be there in a second," she said confidently. I relaxed and obeyed orders, and just like she promised, by the time I shut the door, there they were. Dad was in his black jacket. And Mom in her favorite red blouse and a black pinstriped skirt. They both looked very professional today.

They both get in the car, and we were off. Well, not for long. My bus stop is less than two blocks away, but I still enjoyed the time in the car. As we pulled up, the line was already wrapped around the block, figuratively speaking of course; but it was long, and I'm not that patient, so I bid my hasty farewell.

"Bye, Mom. Bye, Dad. Have a great day at work!" I said through their window.

"We will, we love you!" they said in unison looking back, with Dad's deep bass voice, and Mom's lighter alto voice; it sounded like a symphony.

"I love you too!" I said hastily as I was running toward the bus stop. *Why didn't I look at them! Why didn't I hug them one last time!* I felt so empty remembering it. Then I realized the officers were staring at me in an odd fascination; slowly, I felt my cheeks, which were moist with hot tears. Ooh.

Feeling humiliated, I tried to make an excuse to leave.

"Are you going to take me after school? It would be nice to say good-bye to everyone," I asked.

"No, we need to leave as soon as possible," one said. My eyes were too blurry to see the name tag, but it looked like it said Tim.

"Okay, but can I collect my belongings?" I asked them, feeling a new batch of tears welling up in my eyes.

"Umm…" The officer looked uncertain but still said, "Sure, will ten minutes be enough time?" I smiled gratefully, unable to speak. "Okay, can you meet us back in the office?" asked the officer. I nodded my head again and left.

Surprisingly, it had taken longer than expected. Sixth period was already halfway over, so I went to my locker in a rush, grabbed my things, and stuffed it in my backpack. I took everything, even the picture of my parents; it took everything I had not to start crying again when I looked at it.

Then I was off to my sixth period class to pick up my instrument—ah the violin, I really loved it. When notes lined up, it almost felt like a message or someone whispering in your ear; but they speak through music. Like if it were piano, with multiple eighth notes and the staccato symbol above, it was urgent; something for my ears only. But if it were forte, it was like a speech. It was fun making up words to my music even though the only place it was heard was in my head.

Anyways, as I approach the door, I stop to gingerly check my face for loose tears; it seemed good enough, and so I turned the handle and walked in. I kept my head bowed, so no one could see my puffy eyes. Andrew turns to me as I walk past him.

"Bay, why are you so late?" he asks earnestly. I look up to reply, and he seems taken aback; silently, he sets his viola down, stands up, and walks me to the corner of the room—a good spot for a secret conversation. We were partially hidden by unused stands and a pile of Brocken bows and strings.

"Okay, what's wrong?" he asked softly. I couldn't speak. "Bay, are you in trouble?" he asks. I shake my head. "Then what is it?" he asked, still calm and patient.

"My parents…gone," I seemed to stutter. I must've said more since his eyes grew wide; and he seemed to understand now.

"Oh, Bay! I'm so sorry!" he says in a whisper and wraps me in an awkward hug, but I accepted it gratefully. It felt nice that I could lend some of my worries to him; it made me feel less alone, and at the moment, I really needed that.

Still sniffling, I tell him the rest—about the cloth and beads and about being taken in by my grandma—

who unfortunately has to live in Oregon, which is super far away from Idaho. Yet he took it in, in respectful silence. We were still hidden behind the stands in the far corner of the room, but as I listened, the mindless squeals of strings seemed to subside; and I knew I had to leave, if only I could stay a few more minutes…to say my good-byes. I will try to Skype them, I promise myself, that was the only thing that kept me from another crying fit, I turn back to Andrew.

"I have to go. I'll miss you," I said with a new wave of tears welling in my eyes. He wraps me in another hug, this time more meaningful and less awkward.

"Do you think I could go with you? Like, to the police station?" he asks, suddenly pulling apart from the hug. The thought seemed inviting, but the odds were most likely against it. It already seemed odd that I was going to meet my grandma at the police station. Why not at my house? It's not like I can't survive for a couple of hours alone, still I found my lips forming the words.

"The worst thing they can do is say no, right?" At this, he smiles and maybe my life won't be totally broken.

"Exactly," he says finally.

The next thing I know is I'm explaining everything to Ms. Hawthorn, the orchestra teacher, she gives me and Andrew a "*this is not a game, be respectful*" look and gives us a pass; something inside me feels like it's being pulled toward the end of the hall where the office is.

We got to the office right before my time was up; I look up at Officer Tim and take a shaky breath.

"Can I please bring my friend Andrew? It would make me feel a lot better, and he can call for someone to pick him up," I say, looking up expectantly; for some reason, he seemed to relax.

"Your name is Andrew Nedson, right?" he asks almost gleefully, and for a second, I could've sworn the pupils of his eyes turned red. Andrew seemed taken aback, but Tim waved off the conversation and motioned to the car. *Well, that's as good of a yes as it's going to get*, I think; and hand in hand, we walk out to the police car.

The drive took way longer than expected, but I was really thankful for the extra time with Andrew. He seemed sweeter and sweeter every time I thought about it, at the same time, I was trying to block out the thought of leaving him and all my other friends, and possibly for good. It's going to be so different in Oregon. Andrew leans over to my ear and whispers, "No matter what…we will keep in touch, I promise," he said genuinely. *Why!* Why did you have to make me feel like this!?! Right before I have to leave, I felt like sobbing; but at the same time, it seemed to calm me. I felt like I was being torn apart. He slowly put his arms around me, and I leaned into his shoulder, trying hard to remember everything.

Out of nowhere, our car swerves; and as if Andrew had expected it, his other hand whips from around my shoulders and covers my head as we're T-boned by another car. My head is in between my legs and his hands are over our heads protectively. The car rolls on its side, then on its other side. The only thought in my mind was "*Oh dear God, I am flying through the air!*"

So many spins went by I couldn't even count, and I felt sick, like I'm going to puke all over everyone sick. Slowly but surely, the once police car comes to a stop, upside-down of course. It looked as though the car got in a fight with monster trucks. Andrew's hands came down, and he unbuckled his seat belt. He fell headfirst into the hood—err, floor, whatever—but it was the weirdest thing; his hands automatically are at his head before he even lands, as if they were there the whole time. *Okay, great! So far, my parents are gone. I just barely survived a car crash...and now, I'm going crazy! That's exactly what I needed!* I felt like screaming.

All the adrenaline and fear seemed to turn into boiling rage. If I remember correctly, I ripped off my seat belt, fell headfirst into the hood/floor—without super human awesome moves—and then I'm out of the car. That's when I think of Tim. Where did he go? I looked in the window although hard to see through the cracked glass. No one was there. *What?*

I forget that quickly as I meet Andrew; he was on the side of the road checking for nonexistent wounds. His shirt was in tatters, but that was the worst. I sat down beside him and did the same, my jacket wasn't even salvageable. I threw it on the ground beside me and let out a huff, other than that there was nothing serious I concluded and then turned to Andrew

"Andrew!" I say, suddenly remembering Tim and the other police officer again; he seems to understand without me finishing. In a flash, he was standing up looking up the street. Both of us were thinking we were going to find two police officers on the road with broken necks. What do we see? That's right, nothing!

Something felt wrong. The hairs on the back of my neck stood on end, and without warning; as I turn around. There, there were the two officers with something in their hands; suddenly, Andrew thrust his hand out, trying to swipe away the weird cloth object, but it was little use. Within seconds, they were thrust into our faces. It smelled sickly sweet mixed with something like bleach, and before I knew what it was, everything went black.

TIMMY THOMPSON

"Wake up!" yells Olivia. Why do schools have to be on Thursday? Couldn't they be on Tuesdays, Wednesdays, and Fridays? That way you can take out the two worst days of the week. That would be nice.

"Timmy...Wake up!" Olivia says loudly. She's now peering over me.

"Get out of my room!" I yell back.

"I would, but we're going to be late! And you won't wake up unless I watch you get out of bed," she says with annoyance.

"Fine," I say, too tired for an argument on my laziness

"Good, I will be downstairs. We leave in ten. Unless you want to run to school," she says as if the idea would be perfect. It might be perfect...for her. But we lived about thirteen miles from school, and our school bus is known for coming early and not waiting.

"Okay, now get out!" I say in a suppressed yell.

"Fine, see yah," she said, probably happy to be able to bug me. I almost yelled down the hall how annoying she was, but she would only like that. Time for school. I pick out a clean shirt from the pile on the floor and finish getting dressed. I brush out my brown longish hair and put some new contacts in over my dark blue eyes.

In record time, I run downstairs were there on the table is some toast with strawberry jam. Okay, normally, I wouldn't eat whatever that is; but today, I felt too tired to make something for myself. I should be grateful that for once Olivia made me breakfast. I scarf the toast like a savage dog, chug the milk…and I hate milk, and turn to get my shoes on. Standing right behind me is Olivia, great.

"Jeez, for someone who just got up, you look goooood!" I hear Olivia say. Since when is Olivia nice? *Just take it, its not like you get them often.*

"Hey, thanks," I reply

"Thanks for what?" asks Olivia. Now she's gonna make me say it?

"You know... about me looking good."

"You look like crap with a really bad hair day," she says unhappily.

Huh? "When did you get so touchy when it comes to my hairstyles and apparel?" I ask genuinely; she, however, rolls her eyes.

"Since when have you dressed like a homeless person?" she says. Ouch, that was a burn.

"Whatever, this is the style," I say.

"No, it's not. And, you know why I know that Timmy? Because I'm officially in your grade level now," she states with a mixture of delight and anger. Darn it, I always forget that. She is like the geekiest person in the whole world, and last year, she was so smart that her teacher recommended trying to skip a grade, she did, and well she excelled at that grade too. Now she's in my year group, doing better than me in like…every subject, including lunch.

"I choose not to, frankly," I say dismissively, grabbing my hat and sweatshirt and stuff my backpack with my binders.

"Are we going or not?" I say, trying to change the subject.

"Yeah, let's go," she says, thankfully not putting up a fight.

"So…Mom's gone already?" I ask, recalling the meeting she had pretty early.

"Yeah, we'll have to walk it," she said unenthusiastically.

"So…we better take an umbrella," I said, looking outside.

"No, walking will take too long," she says, annoyed.

"But you just said!" I say, not catching on.

"Wow, you really don't like Thursdays, huh," she says, irritated.

"What?" I ask. Sure I'm slow in the morning, but I'm not stupid.

"We missed the bus smarty pants," she says. I look at the clock, oh crap.

"So what's your brilliant plan, dear sister of mine?" I say with sarcasm spilling off my lips.

"We're going to take the trail," she says like no big deal, whereas I can only stare at her in disbelief. *Was she crazy?*

"The bike trail that I fell on and broke my arm?" I ask, feeling a shudder at the memory.

One year ago the same thing happened. We were going to be late to school, and we decide to go on this trail that we sometimes walk on in the summer. We tried to bike it, hoping it would shave ten minutes off our commute. Well, it didn't. The trail was full of debris and holes where old trees used to be; now there are roots that stick up and scratch at your ankles.

When I was riding behind her, she sent some type of stick that got in my bike chain; the bike turned sharply, then stopped so abruptly I didn't have enough time to yell before I was falling down a steep hill full of poison ivy; thinking about it, they probably saved my life because by the time I reached the bottom of the hill, I had slowed down enough to avoid the jagged rocks in the stream.

I still remember my bone jarring out of my skin and the extreme agony and the rash of the poison ivy. I remember the wave of nausea and how I got sick all over my clothes; Olivia refused to help me after that because of the stink, but the worst part, there is no cell service. We were just lucky enough that there was a man jogging who could get help while Olivia stayed with me. It took two hours for help to come—he was a really out-of-shape jogger—but the pain killers were worth it.

What if that happens again?

"It won't happen again," she says almost like she was reading my mind.

"Fine, but I have an important...project," I lie. "And it will get ruined if I bring it on the bike," true. I did have an important project, but it wasn't due for another week, she didn't know that though since it wasn't in her *advanced class(s).*

"You're totally bluffing," she said. *How did she call me out so fast?*

"How would you know?" I ask. This only makes her looked worried, something was wrong. But I am still too tired to deal with it. After school, I promise myself. "Anyways, I can't bike since I hurt my ankle in PE," I say. That was more believable, right?

"You're lying again!" she says, annoyed. Come on, think!

"Well, I have a doctors appointment, remember?" Which was half true since it was after school, but she didn't know that.

"Yeah, right," she says.

"I do!"

"Sure, maybe later, but now you're lying again!" she remarks. *How was she doing this!?*

"So are you wimping out?" she asked, changing the subject and taunting me in doing it. How does she do it!

I've never been brave, but I know I will regret it if something happens to her and I'm not there.

"Fine, get your bike. I'll meet you outside," I say, trying to get one last minute to take a deep breath before facing my newfound phobia.

"Okay, but make it quick," she said.

I packed my bag with the spare first aid kit, the usual spare coat (I'll explain later), and put some Advil and a water bottle just in case; though this was risky, since if the school catches you with so much as a cough drop, you're suspended. But I didn't want to take chances. *Okay, I think I'm ready.*

I meet Olivia outside; she didn't have her helmet on, but instead was wearing a waterproof hat covering her short brown hair. She has a neon waterproof jacket on too, but it was more like a shell, and it was about as warm as not having one in the first place.

"Let's get this over with," I mutter, and we're off. The ride to school normally would be fifteen minutes, but since there are a lot of crosswalks that when you have to cross the street, you have to get off your bike and push the stupid button, then wait like ten minutes for the walk sign. The trail on the other hand was a trail that leads straight to our school; it cuts our ride in half, but it's a more difficult ride.

About five minutes have passed, so far so good; this time I'm in front, which made me feel better, but also was unnerving. Every time I went through the mud, or over a stick, I could just imagine it flying and hitting Olivia. We were coming to the home stretch, which basically meant the hardest part of the trail; it makes the first five minutes of torture look like easy cruising. I look back at Olivia.

Wait.

"OLIVIA!" I scream as loud as I can; she wasn't there. I didn't even hear her fall. Did she lag behind? I turn my bike around and start riding back, which was a big mistake, because it's almost harder getting back than it is getting over. Eventually, I drop my bike and start to peer over the side of the trail; I was looking for that neon jacket.

Five minutes later, I see bright pink. I run down the trail ignoring the poison ivy and the sticks. I almost trip over a log, and that's when I realize that the log was Olivia. Her jacket had ripped off and flown farther down the hill; she was covered in blood. I couldn't tell where it all came from, but one thing was apparent. *She was in bad shape.*

Now, Olivia might have most of the brains, but one thing she hates is medicine, which so happens to be my strong suit. I think it's so interesting how every day the human body still can surprise everyone.

As I look at her now, I know she's going to need some serious help, and that a miracle would be much appreciated. I bend down examining closer; I notice that she had a three-inch gash underneath all the matted hair and blood. She was unconscious, and her breathing was small unsteady, jagged breaths.

"I got my work cut out for me then," I say miserably.

I try to push my worries away; they only made me mess up, not like I did or anything. First I wiped the blood from her face and arms; her legs seemed fine. She had a broken arm though; this was the grossest part. Knowing that if I didn't set the bone within twenty-four hours the bone would start to mend itself and could create permanent damage. Plus, setting the bone while she was unconscious would definitely reduce the screaming; it could also mean serious infections or internal bleeding. In the end I decide to wait it out. If no one comes by then I will set it.

Now those unfamiliar with medicine should learn this stuff! But if you don't know what it is, basically you have to move the bone back to its original place; hopefully it was a clean break, and I'm not lodging bone fragments into her nerve tissue, or worse, into her brachial artery, which could cause her to bleed to death. And as much as I would love to be an only child again, the risks were really high.

Instead I work on her right arm, and just my luck; she has a stick that goes right through it. *Crap*, I think to myself. I found tears running down my cheeks at one point. I stop and wipe at them before I continue, doesn't do much good though. I start to work on the stick. I don't have an x-ray machine handy, and if the stick is holding an artery from bursting…I'll just leave that one alone, I decide finally; the stick was so unnerving that I end up wrapping it in a loose dressing and continue with my work. Finally, I decide there was nothing more I could do. Her head was in a tighter dressing by the time I was done, and her arms were wrapped up like mummies, one crossing the other over her chest. It worked out pretty good.

Now for the other hard part; I had to either get help and leave her, or I could stay here to make sure she doesn't turn into a bear snack pack and risk being here for days. What could I do? Ah yes, not my best moments for a brilliant plan, so I go on my default mode.

"SOMEONE HELP! MY SISTER'S HURT! HELP US!" I screamed for at least an hour.

"This is just great! I'm stuck here with a mummy for a sister! No, no cell service! And of course this isn't a popular trail! No! That would be way too easy! No, people just like watching me talk to myself!" I scream to no one. I felt so angry at Olivia and so guilty at the same time, which only made me more distressed.

I sat beside her. Three hours had gone by. I ate my apple from my lunch bag—that was the first thing that would go bad, I thought to myself, starved. Olivia was still out for the count, but I managed to slip some water in her mouth without her choking and dying. That was a bonus. I was getting tired, but I knew I had to make sure that nothing came near.

It's getting dark, and knowing there won't be anymore joggers out, I decide to set Olivia's bone. Now this was all without gloves. So blood was all over my hands, which would be more worrisome for Olivia, but still, all the bacteria on my hands could give her some nasty infections and vice versa. Later, I make a makeshift tourniquet with her old jacket and a stick. It wasn't working well, but it seemed to reduce some blood flow. I checked for any wood slivers, but I didn't see any. I put some Neosporin on it and wrapped it again in a tight gauze bandage held together with medical tape.

Afterwards, I wanted to start a fire. I put some kindling and semidry leaves; it had been raining all day, which made it really hard to find leaves as dry as the ones I found. I laid them in a small circle while I tried to use my house keys and a rock to get a spark. It didn't work. Let's keep it at that. Then I remembered a Boy Scout trick. I took the batteries out of my now useless cell phone and try to catch a spark that way; it takes a couple tries, but soon enough, I get a puny fire going, just enough to keep some of the dampness from seeping into me.

That's when I realized Olivia must be cold; heck, I was freezing, and I had my super heavy coat on; she didn't have hers anymore! I used it for the tourniquet! I run to my backpack, which is only one leap away. I look in. I always kept a spare jacket, don't ask why, but I do. The one I was wearing was heavier, so I take it off and put it on Olivia while I took the lighter one. Thankfully it wasn't raining anymore, but the ground was still in puddles; it was dreadful.

Now as you can imagine, every little sound felt like a canon sounding, at times little mice would run by the camp fire with their long shadows. At least twice I screamed like a girl thinking it was a bear or coyote.

That's when I see it. Two red dots. What was that? I shrink into my jacket. Oh please don't be a bear, please, please, please! I think almost weeping, but for some reason, I am perfectly still. That's when the dots began to take form; it looked like a human's silhouette. The red dots disappear and are replaced with two perfectly normal brown eyes. It was a person! I jump up and run to the person. Without thinking, I hug him; he does nothing. I pull apart and look at him frowning at me, but I don't notice anything unusual.

"Please...please, help my sister!" I nearly yell at him, but he stands there with that same unhappy frown.

"Please, go to the police and tell them that Timmy and Olivia Thompson are stuck down here, please!" I say. That triggers some emotion, but instead of a "Yeah, okay, pal," or an "Okay, stay put," he shoves his arm out at me. He was holding something, it was a—then everything went black.

I wake up in a chair. Am I in a hospital chair? I try to get up, and that's when I realize I'm tied to it, that man kidnapped me! Wait, where's my sister? I hope he didn't take her…Well then, she would be alone in the forest, but if she were here—never mind.

"Timmy?" I hear the familiar sound of Olivia's voice; I almost didn't want to look. The last time I had seen here she was covered in dry blood with a broken arm and blue lips from the cold night air and the mummy wrappings I had used to keep bacteria out and hopefully keep her from moving and hurting herself even more. What will she look like? I held my eyes back; maybe she's just muttering things in her sleep, not likely, but anything to keep me from looking.

"Timmy!" Olivia's voice came again with authority, but I still try to ignore her. I pretended I didn't hear her; it didn't work.

"Timmy Thompson, look at me and tell me what's going on," she said angrily. Slowly, I look over at her, but when I did, I didn't see the mummy Olivia; no, I saw the perfectly normal Olivia in her bright neon jacket, not a rip or tear, as if nothing ever happened. This is getting weird.

JESSICA RISE

Ah, the great outdoors! Currently the sun was at its peak, filling the woods with light; this was the one thing I liked about school. This was better than sports, Girl Scouts, and better than math by at least one hundred times. Science, we are currently in our geology unit. Our science teacher, the coolest guy ever, Mr. Sean, knows how to explain it so everyone understands. No sports terms or geeky ones either. Short simple and to the point.

Since we're ending our geology unit, he's sending us all on an outdoor scavenger hunt. We find a rock that we think has the right mineral, we put it in a bag, and when we get all of them, we return to class. Kids who finish before class ends get candy. See? He's the perfect teacher!

I should probably talk about me for a sec, huh? Well, I'm a little clumsy, and it shows with my short choppy blond hair—hey, I only had scissors and a bathroom mirror, you gotta give me some slack here—and my scratched up hands and knees don't exactly keep it secret. Besides that, I have amber-colored eyes, symmetrical features, and a small scar that cuts through part of my right eyebrow; a story that isn't worth sharing if you know what I mean.

Now as I'm outside enjoying the air and finding the rocks with my partner Henry; we've been best friends since like…ever. He is average height, has short black hair and dark, dark brown eyes. And he definitely knows his stuff, which I'm grateful because the day seemed so glazed over; I was too busy taking in the woods while he found the rocks, and this teamwork worked downright awesome, so we were done in five minutes flat—not that I would brag.

So what else to do than wander and talk about vacation plans? We are thirteen; we basically do whatever we want anyway.

"So how about we wander down into triple D territory?" I say, feeling like an adventurer; he turns and looks at me appalled.

"Do you realize that triple D stands for dead, dreary, dump?" he asks, his voice was a very loud and seemingly upset whisper. I rolled my eyes hoping it would translate as *No duh!* A girl can only try, but really, teachers just name it that so students don't wander off in outdoor lessons; sometimes teachers can be really stupid, like everyone knows anything with death in it is like a kid magnet.

"We would get in trouble!" he said, his voice straining to stay in a whisper.

"Only if they catch us," I say, more confident than I felt. I've always been the leader type, but Henry can always find my weak spot.

"Well I'm not taking that chance!" he says.

Oh, please! I've known you all your life. You wouldn't let me do anything alone! You're just trying to scare me, I wanted to say, but I switched it to "Okay then, see you in class!" And with great bounds, I leap off into the woods. Five, four, three, two, one, zeeeeeeeeeeeerrrrrroooooooooooo...wait, he actually isn't gonna come? No, he's got to! *Henry, you better get down here right now you little—*

"Wait up!" I hear him shout from behind me; he's not the sporty type, but he would never admit it. He was running at about a third of my speed, and he was already staggering. I started to pace backwards a bit, finally meeting somewhere in the middle.

"So off to triple D territory then?" I ask, becoming amused.

"I guess so…But only for a minute!" he seems very certain on this point.

"Fine, I'll put it on my timer," I say annoyed. I decide to put two minutes on my watch. *No big deal*, I think to myself.

"Okay," he says, trying to convince himself more than signify that he was ready.

"Off we go…and the timer starts…now," I say.

In silence, we walk at a speedy pace around the piles of garbage and wood; it seemed like this was pretty much it. I checked my watch, and one minute had passed, but as you know it was set for two.

"Wow! Look at that!" I say, looking up from my watch; it was a hole, and it had a diameter of about ten feet and was so deep I couldn't see the end even with my little penlight.

"Here," he says and throws a penny down the hole while I watch the timer; I waited and waited.

"Okay, that is one really deep hole," he said with interest; on the other hand, I was ready to look at some more rocks! No? Well, I had to try.

"See, I told you this place was going to be cool. Oh, the timer went off. Do you still want to head back?" I say, hoping his newfound interest wouldn't tramp over his phobia of doing anything bad. Plus, that hole was starting to give me the creeps.

"Hold on, I want to see when it ends," he said on his hands and knees leaning toward the hole listening for the sound of the penny.

"You probably didn't hear it. Come on, let's get out of here. I want to get that smarty he promised the winners," I said with more haste than the last time. Startled, he looks up. I was startled too. When have I ever been scared?

"Sure, okay fine," he says, slowly starting to get up without mentioning the fear in my tone. That's when the hairs on the back of my neck stand on end as I hear the distinct crunch of dry leaves and snapping twigs.

Henrys eyes go wide like an owl's. My hands nervously play with my hair; I was trying to pretend I didn't notice whoever was behind me. I wasn't really good at it.

"JESSICA!" he screams, looking at something over my shoulder. I feel frozen with fear. I turn around. A man in a black ski mask has his hands wrapped around a long thin knife—definitely not a butter knife—and only his eyes were visible from the mask; and as I look into them, determining the intent he had for the knife in his hand, his eyes turned red.

I blink, and they were back to normal; it must be from all this fear I think hastily. It was only a second that we stood in that stare down, and then he took a step towards me. He thrust his knife at me, no doubt aiming for my stomach…or my throat.

I jump back avoiding the blade by a centimeter at most, but as I jump back, Henry, still on his hands and knees, trips me; soon enough, I'm falling.

I close my eyes waiting for a hard land. That's when I get a sinking feeling; I was falling down the hole! I hear Henry screaming, but I realized it wasn't from outside the hole. I look up; I see Henry a few inches above me. He was blocking out the light from the hole opening. With all the adrenaline I had, I could've grabbed Henry and flew out. Instead, I look up.

"You don't think it's possible that this will lead to China, and we can learn Chinese and eat a lot of rice, do you?" I yell up. Henry screams stop, but he doesn't respond. I don't blame him. The hole felt endless, like the one that Alice fell through in the book *Alice's Adventures in Wonderland.* Wouldn't that be nice, to just wake up, that this was all a dream? No such luck. Thinking the end was near, I try to move to the sides of the walls. Luckily, Henry catches on and does the same.

I try to grab at the roots of old trees. Really, I was just trying to get a hold. One thing crossed my mind, *Even if we do survive…how do we get out?* That sends a shiver through my whole body. *I have to do this*, I reassure myself. *Come on, one step at a time.* A breeze blows through my jumbled thoughts. Okay, step one, get ready; feet down, slightly spread apart, check. Step two, lightly run hands along the wall. When something sturdy comes, hold on for dear life.

This was hard, but eventually, I get hold of a branch. I knew it could break at anytime, but I felt frozen. Soon enough though getting through my fear, so painfully slow, I start scaling the moist mossy—a total pain to climb up—wall. That was when I notice Henry wasn't beside me, but he was, I could've sworn it! He had gotten a branch before me, but when I looked up…not there either.

"HENRY!" I scream, tears filling my eyes; I start to choke on my sobs when I don't hear a reply.

"HENRY!" I yell again, this time at least twice as loud, this time I hear something, it was faint, but distinct.

"Let go," came his voice beside me.

"NO!" I screamed, tears streaking my face. I look to my right, then to my left again, but just like the last time he wasn't there.

"Let go. We won't die."

"How is that even possible?" I exclaim confused. My hands were in a constant aching pain like they were being pulled apart very slowly; I was weeping so hard that my whole body was shaking. My hands kept slipping yet, at the same time, couldn't move; it was a wonder that I was still holding on.

I wouldn't give up. I couldn't! Who was he to tell me to jump to my certain death! Wait. If he were falling, wouldn't his voice be getting softer?

"I don't know…just trust me," he said.

"Wait, Henry, where are you?" I yell as loudly as possible.

"Let go," he urges me again, not giving me the answer I had hoped for.

Urg! So it was either stay alive or die trusting him. Hmm…yeah, I'm going to go with choice A! Trying to forget him, I start climbing again. But it only got harder and harder. Soon the wall was so slick I had to dig my hands into the muck that was sadly the wall. More than once, my handhold would break or disappear, like trying to climb a wall made up of loosely packed dry sand. Eventually, after what felt like hours, climbing up the wall became impossible; I felt the full weight of my body pulling me in the other direction. *Oh please make it quick*, I think with every muscle screaming in agony.

I let go, I fall, and again I feel like I'm on a roller coaster going straight down; with my hands on my stomach, I silently say my good-byes. I fall feet first, which was a mistake; my stomach jumps in my throat and makes me feel dizzy on so many levels. Trying to forget the weird sensations, I try to remember all the good times I had, like when I went on my first canoe; it wasn't the best time, seeing that it tipped and I almost drowned.

Or when I made my first fire. It was a candle, and it burned all my eyebrows and eyelashes off; yeah, I was a really stupid toddler, but they were good times.

And my favorite memory: when I successfully put up a tent, especially since my other tries had turned the little poles into fully loaded whips that hurt worse than the time I broke my arm on the seesaw—Don't even ask.

But the last memory, and by far one of the shortest and less painful memory, will be the time looking for rocks, in the forest, in North Carolina on the nicest day of the season for the coolest teacher in the world with my best friend, Henry. Yeah, that's definitely a good one. But now, as I fall, I realize Jessica Rise and Henry Tucker will die; at least, I tell myself, it will be together.

I could hear Henry's breathing. Either I'm falling way faster than he is, which is unlikely, or…the ground is really close. I close my eyes waiting for my imminent death; I kept squeezing my eyes for a bit longer, the sensation in my stomach subsides, and I feel like I am levitating. Wait, breathing? Is it really Henry's breathing? But he…he…

I open my eyes then; I'm in a room, a box with no hole in the ceiling where we could've fallen through. How'd I get here? I look to my left and gave a silent sigh of relief. Sitting beside me was Henry. Still when I tried to get up to hug him, to laugh and say we were alive just like he promised, yep, that's right, I was tied to a chair. I feel like an *I told you* so moment is coming...

I look at him helplessly, then I look around and so are all the other people. How did I get here? Wait, did I black out? Then something dawned on me…am I dead? If I were, this was definitely not how I imagined heaven. To make sure, I kick the chains around my feet with all my might, and with a reassuring splicing pain through my leg, I lay back on the chair; whatever happened, I'm alive, Henry's here, and other than my leg that I just kicked, I feel fine.

Save what happened for later, I think to myself, enjoying the absence of extreme physical labor. *'Cause seriously, who has fallen into a bottomless pit, tried to climb out when it was as slick as a waterslide and with the same number of handholds too! That and to basically give up thinking you would die, all but to land in what looks like some metal conference room... This is either the best or worst day of my life!* I think, still confused but happy.

STAN PRICE

Three days ago, it was life as we liked it on the police force in the big CA. It was great, at least till that radio call. At first, it seemed like an average call, downtown San Francisco, domestic violence. So E. J. and I turned on the sirens and sped down the street; we were there in nearly five minutes. When we got there though, that's when everything started.

"Yeah, domestic violence, right," E. J. muttered under his breath, clearly irritated.

"Come on, let's just see what we can do," I say, trying to hide my anger as well.

"Whatever, man, this is totally bogus," says E. J. in a controlled whisper.

The place was a dump; it was clearly abandoned and had a god-awful smell. *Who in their right mind would call this a domestic violence?* I think grumpily as I jog up to Jen, a patrol officer same as me, only she's been working here for much longer. If you don't know the ropes around this place by day 2, obviously you haven't met Jen yet. She's tall, with graying hair, and subtle wrinkle lines around her face; she almost looks like a grandmother trying to play the good cop–bad cop part, and let me tell you, there is nothing scarier than having Jen play bad cop, nothing.

"You sure this is domestic violence?" I start. "What happened here? It looks abandoned," I say. This place is officially giving me a weird feeling; I just wanted to get this over with so I can get out of here.

"No one's sure about squat around here. I've lost communications with chief, and right now, we're looking at a possible homicide and a meth lab explosion. We won't know for sure, but Steve is looking at the street tapes and should be back any time no—" She was interrupted by the sound of sirens; a cop car came swerving in the lot, raising all the dust into one massive cloud. Two officers I didn't know came out loaded with P99s, a bit uncommon for officers, but this day was a bit uncommon too. *It's probably nothing, maybe its standard in their unit…no big deal*, I try to convince myself. But something was wrong in his stance; you could tell he was nervous. His brow was furrowed in concentration, like he was confused. *What the heck was going o—*

"Officer Price, you are under arrest for the murder of Madeline Roseberry and for property damage," he says loudly while approaching me with a pair of handcuffs.

"Whoa, hold on! He was doing other stuff with me over on main street," said E. J., recovering first unlike me who was staring with my mouth gaping. The officer who announced my arrest just sighed.

"Officer Tanner, you were also seen on the footage at the scene with Officer Price. You and Price are going to a federal jail until you see a judge for your sentence," he said with a forced calmness, his gaze still on me; then he started to approach us.

Finally recovering, I look at E. J. He looks stunned now. Then I look back at the officer. "Wait, you mean the street tape Steve was analyzing? Why'd he send you? How do you know it was us on the tape?" I ask truly puzzled; my mind buzzing with questions.

"Steve was analyzing it, at least until the FBI took it over. We matched up the two faces on the tape with everyone in the database. Yours were the only ones that matched…that and the car in the tape had your license number," he said with a smirk that I wish I could slap right off his face, and for the slightest of moments, his eyes seemed to turn red, just the pupils—must be the sun, I think.

"Wait a second, you're part of the FBI? What for!? I think we deserve to see some ID," I say upset. *This can't be right*, I think, confusion sweeping over me. "Look, I have my orders and wish you both would comply peacefully. Anything you say or do may be used against you in court," he replies, showing his ID badge yet completely ignoring my first question. "You have a right to a lawyer…," he continued, but my mind was already buzzing with the different possibilities; he took a deep breath and handcuffed us.

"This is bogus! We were set up! I don't even know Madeline what's-her-face!" I shout, my hands feel unusually hot—no, wait. My cuffs do, they feel on fire! I look down at them, and they are glowing red. *Okay, what is going on today!?* I try to wave them around to cool 'em off, which actually helps till the two FBI guys stuff us into their car.

Handcuffing a person is second nature to me; well, it would be the same for you after two years, I would hope. But I never thought I would see the day when I, would be riding in the *backseat* of a cop car.

In the backseat, E. J. was fidgeting; he never could keep still. I guess that's what makes him such a good fighter. But this was different, he was like a caged animal being crowded by a mob; guess he never thought he would be doing this either. It smelled like cigarette smoke and air freshener throughout the whole car. It was hot, and if you haven't noticed already, the nearest federal jail was way out of town, at least an hour away; and by how fast we were going, which was like ten miles under the speed limit, we weren't going anywhere soon.

At the facility two and a half hours later, we were checked for any weapons. Sometimes I just don't get people. When I walked in the building, I could name almost everyone, and now they were treating me like any other criminal. *No, Hi, good to see you, huh,* I thought sadly.

As I walk through the metal detector, an officer with a grim look on his face gave me the standard orange jumpsuit, then me and E. J. were escorted to cell B-1102; it was on the first floor and had a beautiful view of the dumpster. *Not only am I accused of murder, but I get to smell the dumpster for another week*, but that's the weirdest part…If E. J. and I weren't there until the radio call, how were our faces on that video and our license number? Whoever wanted to set us up really wanted it to look bad...on us.

One whole day has gone by, and to be honest, I need to give some credit to the people who live here. The cell that I'm sharing with E. J. is a rectangle smaller than my bathroom, and I have a small bathroom. The beds were basically concrete blocks with sheets and that's an understatement, and lastly, the room is like an oven set to preheat with a bunch of trash and stuff in it; the smell could've easily knocked me out if I had just come in. Even the officers guarding our door seemed to have crept a few feet away.

I snuck a peek at E. J. He was trying to pace the room and failing miserably, every once in a while he would start mumbling to himself, or he would hit his foot on the concrete bed and start swearing like a lunatic, even more than he already did. You could tell he was suffering. He needed out—badly. Every second I watched him gave me another reason to get out. He looked up at me for a second, his face pale white and filthy, even his dark brown hair looked twice as grimy if that's even possible. There were deep worry lines on his forehead, and he had bags under his eyes from a sleepless night in prison. It looked like he was going to go insane in here, and all I could do was watch.

I was pathetic. I couldn't even think of something to say, but what could I say? *I know they think they have our faces in that videotape, and our license plate. But everything's all right as long as we have each other!* Even thinking of it sounded like it was coming from some melodramatic, boring movie.

"Look, bro, just relax. We're innocent. They can't do anything to us," I say calmly—even though I know that if the evidence is against us, judges don't exactly like the scout's honor stuff. He looks into my eyes and stops pacing; that in itself is a leap of progress. His eyebrows turn up, and silent tears leak out, leaving clean streaks over his dirty face. This is the first time in two years on the job I have seen him cry. It was really unnerving.

"Why would someone frame us? Like they must've gone through a lot to do this, but why us?" he said shakily through tears. I sucked in my breath; E. J. had voiced the one thing we were both thinking. Why were we so special? Why did they pick us to frame out of everyone else? The wheels in my brain were turning so fast that I couldn't even understand half of what I was thinking; so many questions began to swirl with all the emotions and everything that had happened so far. I couldn't figure out where to begin. I shake my head trying to get rid of the thought.

"Look, let's try and get some Zs. Want to look our best for the judges," I say, avoiding the question and trying to lighten the mood.

"Yeah, whatever you say," he says and jumps onto the concrete bed with a thud. I carefully get onto the bed; even though they are the most uncomfortable thing ever, I fell asleep as soon as I hit the concrete pillow.

I wake up to the smell of smoke. *That's not right*, I think groggily. I open one eye and see the red emergency flashes going. The alarm sounded far off but still loud. I look at E. J. He was still asleep. That's when I take inventory on the room, but what room? As I looked around, the wall leading to the outside was gone, like it was never there in the first place, then the wall to the aisle was gone too. The two walls that were standing were just enough to keep it from falling on top of us.

"E. J., Come on! We need to get out before the walls fall on our sorry butts!" I said in an exaggerated whisper. He opens one eye groggily. "Come on! We don't have much time!" I say, becoming more aware of the creaking in the walls as the seconds tick by. Then his head shoots up off the pillow; fully awake, he registers our surroundings.

"Come on, this way," I say, leading to the aisle of all the cells. I don't want them to think we're trying to escape, that would really look good in front of a judge. That's when I see them, well… when I see us. E. J. number two was carrying a semiautomatic Browning and me number two was carrying a P99. They're running right at us; they look like a perfect replica of us. *This is weird*, I think as they're running towards us. I rub my eyes not quite believing what I was seeing. And when I open them, they're gone. *Huh? Maybe they were just in my imagination*, I think with a sigh of relief. But then hands reach out from behind us; before I can react, they put a cloth over my mouth and nose. It smells like bleach with something. My eyes are growing heavy, and there's a tingling in my arms and legs. I feel numb, and my thoughts slow. Then everything goes dark.

I wake up to a stark black room. I wiggle around in what appears to be a seat. *Where am I?* I can't help but wonder, and that's when I remembered my partner. Is he here?

"E. J., where are you!" I yell loudly. "Are you here?" I ask still getting louder. "E. J., are you all right?" I ask, finally becoming silent; there were only two scenarios I could think of: one, he was never here, or two, he *was* here. But the only thing I could hear was my heartbeat beating in my ears

"Where am I?" I finally scream in frustration because, seriously, I really doubted how much more I could take of this.

"That's exactly what I was about to explain," said a foreign voice in front of me. I sucked in a breath; I *hadn't* expected someone else to be here, but I only felt grief. *Where was E. J.? What's happening?*

Just then the lights turn on; everything bathed in a brilliant white light that felt like being trapped staring at the sun; as my eyes adjusted, I checked out the area. That's when I saw them. We were in some type of metal conference room, except there were no desks. Just twelve chairs—including mine—in a semicircle facing a television screen. In the chairs were kids, teenagers, no one over eighteen though. Most are still asleep, some just awakening, then there were others that were just too shocked to speak.

LILIA RIDER

"Who are you?" I ask, worry kicking me hard in the stomach. *Why me?* was just itching to escape my lips.

"My name is Eric Nova, you can call me Eric," said the man on the screen in a smooth even voice like a lullaby.

"But *who* are you? Why are we here? And why have us tied down if you're not even here?" I say a bit annoyed.

"Ah yes, I am a scientist at NASA. I work on a classified unit. As for the reason you're here, to put it simply, you're going to save the world," he says as if he saves the world every day. I choke on my next words wondering if I had misheard him. Saving the world? I'm twelve! Isn't this like child abuse?

"Yes, I understand your concern, but this is very well planned. Don't worry, you're more than capable of accomplishing this task" he says with a hint of a smile. He knew something, I just knew it.

"Wait, how would you know? We don't even know what we have to do yet!" I say with rising hysteria.

"Let's just say…we've been watching you, Lilia," he says with true admiration in his eyes.

"Wait, where are you?" asked a boy, probably around thirteen years old. The man smiles broadly.

"I am not alive at this time, so if you would like the right answer, I suggest asking the right question," he says all Yoda–Star Wars like. Who is this guy?

"Then how come I see you? How did you know we are the chosen ones? How did you get us here if you're dead?" he asks. The rapid-fire questions begin to give me a headache, but I had every intent to know what the answers would be.

"Timmy, for your information, I recorded this just a bit after I knew you would be the ones for the task. My responses are voice activated and limited. My voice bots got you here. They are extremely lifelike and are made to accomplish a variety of tasks, some of them you may know as officers, friends, or some might have seemed like strangers. But they were specifically designed to... relocate you at the right time, depending on your environmental situation. Now if only I can fix that infuriating red-eye problem! But enough of this, you will all know what to do soon enough," he says happily. For a moment, a look of confusion crosses his face, but he quickly hides it with a smile. *Huh?*

"So let's say you recorded this a year before we met here," girl with blond hair says and motions toward this room. "And had it set for this day, but how would you know the future now? Like what if someone died before this or something?"

The man's grin only gets bigger. "Time protects itself, Bay. It's the universe we have to deal with," he says knowingly. This only earns puzzled glances around the room; the man sighs and says, "When you think of time, what do you think of?"

Timmy raises his hand, not thinking of his cuffs, which somehow disappeared. "It's a line that goes on forever on both ends," he says. Just then, a small rectangular panel slides open and a whiteboard appears. How Eric could've known he would say that is mystery... maybe it's voice activated? He looks scared at first. Then, seeming to realize he didn't have ropes cuffing his arms and legs anymore; his face twists into a nervous smile, and he walks up to the board and says, "It's a never-ending line showing all of time. It goes on forever both ways."

Another kid raises her hand, not realizing that she too has broken free of her shackles. "Well, if history went on forever, wouldn't it be really boring? I mean, if it were only space and rock forever before the earth and bacteria and evolution stuff, like what's the point of having space forever when there's nothing to fill it?" she says wonderingly.

The boy interrupts her thoughts. "Space didn't go on forever or we wouldn't be here," he says with a contempt look on his face.

"But if the earth was formed around 4.6 billion years ago, then time from then and back go on forever. So time would never get to us, but it did, so then it would be a ray," she continues to explain.

"I like your point, Henry, but let's hear Olivia through, shall we?" Eric intervenes. It almost seemed like a chess match. Whose theory was right? Whose was wrong? And by the looks of it, Henry lost.

"Now the real question is, when did it start?" she says, obviously confused by her own words, then another picture shows up on the board. It was a line with and arrow on one end and a dot on the other—a ray.

"Well, it could be a line that goes on forever," says another kid, "like, think about it, if you went back in time, well that means the past is still going otherwise, you wouldn't be able to live in the past, it would be just a stopped picture, because so this must mean that all the dates are going at once, since you're there, so even though we haven't lived it yet, we might be like the president or something. And same with going backwards, we could be living now and still the world was never made in another time it all depends where you are at. So when you want to go back to your present time, you don't say the future because that could be any date. Yesterday could be the future if you're living the day before yesterday like I said. It really all depends on where you are on the line." Nods go around the room; it even made sense to me—no joke.

"Hmm. Interesting thought, Jessica. But that would be true no matter if time were a line, a ray, or whatever you people come up with," answers Eric.

"I thought time was supposed to be a circle," I blurt out. Everyone turns to look at me, but then, I get it. "If time's a circle, you both would be right because it goes forever, but any point can be the start," I finish, amazed at my point. *Where'd that come from?*

The man named "Eric" smiles ear to ear. We were finally getting somewhere. "Yes, think of time as a circle. Everything has a circle. The life cycle, the water cycle, geometry. All circles," he starts.

"But if time's a circle, what happens when we make a whole loop?" I ask, catching on to his thought.

His smile fades as he sighs. "Well, if you were to pick a time, calling it the starting point of this circle, what would you think the starting point is?"

"The beginning of time," says a man.

"The beginning of humans," says a girl.

"The beginning of earth," says another boy.

Answers come from around the room.

"No, the beginning of life, like living life, not earth, that's dirt, not time, that's another topic, not humans... It's too soon," I say, silencing the crowd of voices.

"Excellent, now think about it, how many mass extinction were there?"

"Depends, some say five, some say eight or nine," said a boy who looks in desperate need of the sun. "Some were worse than others."

"Ah, but how do you know this, Josh?" he says with a grin.

The boy ponders the question only a moment and replies, "The amount of fossils were the amount of deaths, well-preserved deaths anyway, and when there were lots of fossils, that meant lots of deaths, making a *mass* extinction," he says, giving *mass* a lot of emphasis.

"Okay, so if the number of deaths is the number of preserved fossils, could that mean there would be a whole species gone before your scientists could look at them? You know, if they weren't preserved?" says Eric.

"I suppose. It would be unlikely, near impossible almost," he says hesitantly, obviously not liking the idea.

"Now tell me, do scientists know exactly what happened, why all the creatures died?" he says in a teasing tone.

"Well, not exactly, but some have found asteroids, or volcanic rock, that gives us some proof of how they died," he said, still not catching on.

"Now what made the asteroid fall on earth?" he said.

"Umm, I don't know," says the boy, looking weary.

"Well, have you ever thought something made that happen?" he says.

"Of course I have, there's just no proof," says the boy defensively.

"What do you mean no proof? There's proof everywhere!" says Eric, anger flashing in his eyes.

"What are you trying to point out here? It's not like we can just pick the day we save the world and all," I say, irritation and anger sweeping through my body like a virus; Eric straightens and looks at me.

"So like I was trying to say, if we picked the beginning of life as our start, that would be when the whole thing starts to change. Now so far, we have done the really simplified version of it all. Time is multiple things especially a circle. Now think of a cylinder with no top. It's like it's made out of many circles, right? And that means that a mass extinction is the end of time, one loop. Of course, it takes a long time to do this, but when one loop goes, another circle is added. Now these circles make a cylinder, and this cylinder makes a thread. There are about twelve thousand circles, no bigger than an atom molecule, us tiny thread, weaved into the fabric of time, but—"

"Wait, you said twelve thousand circles! And if one means the end…Wait, how do you know this?" says a girl with an insanely high voice full of hysteria.

"Thanks for pointing that out Chelsey..." he says, seeming a bit annoyed that he got interrupted "Does everyone know the story of Roanoke?" He paused while a chorus of nods filtered through the room. "Then you might know the one thing they left us… Croatian. It was a name that was spelled out on the post of the settlement. Everything else was gone. Well, in numerology, the name would look like this." Just then, the whiteboard has a row of numbers. It says, "3, 8, 5, 1, 5, 5, 1, 4."

"Now if you multiply these numbers, what would you get?" says the man.

"Twelve thousand," says another girl.

"Very good, Valery. Now can anyone tell me where these people went?" questions Eric.

"We don't know for sure. Some say they went to Croatian island, some say they got attacked by the natives or joined them, others say they made boats out of the housing and sailed away," says Valery.

"Well, what if I were to say it was another reason entirely?" said Eric, happily confusing everyone.

"Now I have a great, great, and many more greats grandfather. He was a scientist, he wasn't exactly well known, for some of his theories were a bit too advanced to grasp. Anyways, he came to Roanoke. Does anyone know why?" he asks, eager to explain; everyone just shakes their heads or shrugs. "Well, he was there because the circle was thinning there."

"The circle was what? How would he know that?" says a man in his mid-twenties.

"Well, Stan, like I said, time is a circle. These circles add up to threads when they're all stacked up on one another. The life in this galaxy alone has twelve thousand circles to make the thread. Now places in other galaxies have many different-sized threads. These together make a fabric. The fabric is unstable now because every time that time ends, the universe gives one particular creature a chance to fix it, the universe has been looking for the creature who will balance out the fabric for millenniums, but none, until now have succeeded, thus making the fabric uneven and wrinkled. Before, the universe could save one or two creatures they thought would save it the next time, but now the thread is so unbalanced, the universe is destroying the thread rather than fixing it. The fabric is so damaged the universe can't save anyone anymore. Everything will be folded into time and stop. That's all we know will happen so far if we fail. But if we do fail, things will be much worse than any can imagine," Eric says darkly, "as for my many greats grandfather, let's just say he gave us some time before the beginning of the end, but Roanoke had to pay the price."

"Wait, so what happens when the end starts?" says a boy who's been very quiet the whole time.

"Well, remember how I said everything's a circle, and when you make a full loop, that's the beginning of the end?" Eric says almost sheepishly. Nods go around the room. "Well, when a new time starts as it were a line that's following the groove of the last circle, this way the end is always the same distance every time, but when other threads knot around our little thread, sometimes our threads can get smaller or bigger. Now because of another knot, our time is reduced in half and steadily declining. What we have found is when the end meets the beginning, the beginning creates a disaster, wiping out almost all of life, except for those the universe has chosen. And as a result, they get worse every time. Now as we are expecting to go into our next beginning of the end, it will be worse than all recorded history combined, if you can imagine. What I can tell you is that the beginning of the end creates a black hole. We don't know much about this black hole because it will be made by time itself, since the tearing of the fabric will soon become a tangible force. What we do know is that as soon as our time meets that time, the wrinkled fabric collapses, and we are sucked into a black hole, and we will all instantaneously stop. Time, space, life everywhere, everything will be gone." With those last words, everyone starts to speak—shouting, crying, yelling, and spouting ideas, others saying their good-byes. Slowly this information sinks in; for a moment, I'm stunned. It feels as though my heart is growing too big for my chest and is jumping into my throat. I start to wheeze, then as my mind seems to settle, like dust in a dessert, I see it; I understand everything.

"You said time protected itself right?" I say.

"Yes, if nothing were to interrupt it, time would fix itself. But in fact, many things have disoriented it, like the universe in which we base our laws of physics off of, which is also trying to help."

"Isn't that a good thing?" asks Adam Shards, interrupting Eric.

"No, Adam, it certainly is not. Think of it this way, you're working on a project, and you're doing fine, then another person comes with a different way of doing things. Both of you work on the same project doing different things, now think of you, and millions of people, all with different ideas working on one project—yours. And they all did it according to their rules. Would your project be very organized?" Eric asks.

"No," Adam replies quietly. If things weren't so serious, I probably would've laughed at him looking like an idiot in front of everyone.

"Exactly. Now think of time as you and the million other people as the different universes. The fabric of time is so messed up, the only way to save it is to destroy it, and start again," he says, faltering.

"Okay, wait a second here 'Universes?' as in more than one?" asks Valery.

"Yes, yes, yes. We live in a solar system, inside the Milky Way galaxy. Outside that are plenty of other galaxies, and those as a whole is our universe, which makes the circles that add up to our single thread. So there are many, many, many more universes, some just like ours that weave together. And normally this fabric doesn't actually exist, at least not yet. It's becoming so knotted, that as it starts to tear it will instantaneously become a tangible thing. Which in theory will self destruct all the universes in its fabric, leaving nothing."

"So then how do we stop the fabric from becoming real, if it's not real?" I ask, somehow already knowing the answer; like why else would he be telling us this?

"We have a plan," says Eric flatly.

"And we all survive right?" I say, shaking.

Eric begins to smile. "So far, our plan is flawless," he replies, not exactly answering the question.

"So what's the plan?" I ask, eager for an answerer to the madness around me.

"The plan is to let you save the world," he says with a snicker, like we should already have guessed. *Well I guessed that part, you big oaf!* I thought angrily.

"No, I mean, like what are we supposed to do?" I say, clarifying my question.

"Well, you're all smart kids…you can think of something," he says placidly, which of course made me want to scream.

"You mean, you bring us here, wherever this is, tell us the world is going to end, just a bunch of teenagers, scaring us to death, for what? To tell us we need to save the world from a black hole that will stop everything! And instead of getting your top scientists and astronauts and other people, you bring us, right? Because we are the only people in the *whole* world that can save this, this fabric! And since this is such an easy topic, you're just going to let us figure it out on our *own*!" I say, my voice rising with every word, the anger building violently inside me pours out filling each word with enough hate that it felt like a truck driving over my tongue; my vicious attack on Eric silences the complaints of the crowd around us.

"Now why would I choose just a bunch of teenagers unless I knew 100 percent that they could save the world?" says Eric.

"Then why won't you tell us what to do?" I say, my anger vanishing as fast as it began.

"Because If I tell you, we'll screw up time even more than it already is," he said hastily.

"But if we're destroying it, and making a new one, can't we do whatever we want?" I ask angrily.

He smiles broadly. "Looks like you have the what, just get the how, and the rest will follow," he says with one last salutation, meeting all of us in the eyes.

"Wait, who's Madeline Roseberry?" asks the man, Stan I think is his name. Eric looked nervous but answered anyway.

"She was my granddaughter," he says quietly then the screen blinks out and the shackles on our arms and legs are all gone.

"No, wait!" I scream at the blank screen. I almost felt like crying. Why was he doing this to us?

HENRY TUCKER

I had rubbed my wrists raw on the hard metal shackles, and now the cold air stung them like lemon juice. I was breathing heavy; I had to save the world? It felt like the weight of the world was dumped on my shoulders, which technically it was. I was the kind of guy that was reliable, predictable even; it seemed I was average at everything, which is good, but now it felt that all I am got stuffed in a bag, and an imposter was inside me.

I thought of Jessica beside me, she and I were best friends, but now I was beginning to worry about how our friendship was starting to untwine; it was all because I told her to jump, to trust me, even though she could be sitting in triple D crying for me, not worried about the world ending...Was she mad at me for that?

She knew me better than anyone; she knew that I wasn't big on standing out, so she picked up the slack in that area, and she wasn't the best at logical thinking, which was a place I could even the scale a bit, but now... now things felt like they were going to change forever. I just didn't know how much. Just like I had no clue how we were going to save the world.

"Okay, people, we need to figure this out. But first, let's get the easy part out of the way. My name is Jessica, to those who didn't catch my name, and I am thirteen," she said it like a true leader taking control, just like the old Jessica. I breathe a sigh of relief, one less thing I have to worry about.

"My name is Stan, and I'm twenty-two," says a man beside Jessica.

"My name is Chelsey, and I'm fifteen," says a girl with an insanely high voice with way too much pep for this room full of worry.

"My name is Henry, I'm thirteen," I say when the line comes to me.

As the names go on, I notice that there are six girls and six boys ranging from age ten to twenty-two. Was this an accident? He did mention something about converting things to numbers...

"So here is what we know. We know that the world will end if we don't fix it first, and if we don't, there are no second chances. We also know that time is so messed up that it can't be fixed but thrown away and started over. And lastly, the end will happen when we get sucked into a black hole. Any questions?" says Jessica as she looks around. None. "Good, so any suggestions?" she asks, hopefully looking around again. None. Then I have the weirdest idea, an idea that can't possibly be my own; at first, it's a blurry image with some points in focus, as I think harder the image becomes clearer and clearer until it's there, glistening in my mind so clear, simple, easy that it stands out like a fire on a black horizon.

"First, we need to figure out when. Now this is just a guess, but the range of ages here is twelve. I can't say this for a fact, but I think we have twelve days to save the world," I say, a cool poise taking hold of my body making me seem in control and clear minded.

"Okay, so if we have twelve days, what do we do?" says Jessica, obviously fortunate that I said something.

"Well, we know that the world's going to end because of a black hole, so is the earth going to be the center of this black hole? Is it going to come from an already existent black hole? Or is it going to start up at the beginning of the end somewhere else," I say, cold hard logic spilling off my lips.

"Well, he said it was made by fabric itself, so we can take out the earth, and if it were already existent, then NASA would have reported it by now," says Jessica, puzzling over the question.

"I think the sun's going to be the black hole," says a boy named Timmy. *Stay out of my spotlight, kid!* I thought bitterly, but as I thought about it, it fits the image in my mind perfectly *as if he were reading my mind*

"Why's that?" says Jessica, listening attentively.

"Well, he was saying everything revolves around a circle, so the point in the middle of the circle would be the best way to destroy the ring, so if the sun, which is really a star were to explode into a super nova, not only will the matter at the center of its core compress so hard that it would turn into a black hole, but the heat and nuclear waves would demolish our atmosphere, all our water would evaporate to space, and the world would be toast. And if this super nova were big enough, there's a lot more things it would do afterward…or all at once," he finishes.

"What would happen afterwards?" Jessica and I say together.

"Well, the pull of the black hole's gravity would pull everything at it, so if we weren't dead already, we would be crushed by the other planets in the solar system. Our whole galaxy would collapse and anything else that was close enough, and if you think of our galaxy as part of a food chain, even though we aren't being eaten by other galaxies, the pull of our galaxy could be supporting another. And if that were to float off into space, then others could to. So think of it as a domino effect, one goes the rest follow, I bet that the fabric is destroying each of its threads, and then it wouldn't be too hard to destroy time along with everything else," says Timmy solemnly.

"Wait…you said that it might happen all at once?" asked Olivia.

"Well yeah, he, I mean Eric, said that everything as we know it will collapse. So in theory the black hole could be like a tear in the thread, and then it just sucks up the thread too. This could take hours, minutes, seconds…or maybe even less. I don't know."

"But in a way that would be a good thing 'cause we have to start over anyway right?" says Olivia. I ponder the question. Yes, it would because it would definitely destroy time, but how do you destroy time but not destroy it? That's it! It's right in front of us all along.

"Okay, so if the sun were the source of the black hole, how do we stop it? Well, we can't avoid it, can't use guns or missiles because it's gas. But we can fight fire with fire," I say, setting off a round of confused looks.

"So if there's a black hole, we fight it with a black hole," I say, waiting for a response.

"Quick question, isn't that the one thing everyone says not to do? Ya' know 'fire and fire only makes more fire' kinda stuff?" asks Lilia.

"Yeah, wouldn't that just make a bigger black hole?" asked Jessica beside me.

"Well, that's one possibility, or the two black holes gravity will pull them towards each other, and when they reach each other, just seconds before when they are about to join but not entirely, we pass through, the universe I mean. It's perfect!"

"Yeah, if you want to die!" says Stan, annoyed.

"No, no, I mean a wormhole. It's impossible to live through a black hole because the place you're closer to the black hole sucks you in while the other gravity is stretching you the other way, never letting you get through before you are stretched until you die and then you'll go into it and be compressed into nothing, but when two black holes join, there's about a second where the two just meet and its pull won't kill you but will fold the fabric in two and get us out the other end, it'll be like plucking one thread while leaving the other's behind to get sucked into nothing. This is kind of like a onetime deal since time is so messed up all the rules are most likely changing anyways, so then the old wrinkled fabric is gone, just a thread will be growing, without all the universes tangling it. And if we're lucky, these circles will be bigger," I say with a wink, finishing strong.

"That could just maybe work," Jessica said.

"So in twelve days, the sun will go into a super nova and the earth will end, so we have to make another black hole before that happens. And if we do this at the right place, at the right time, then the two black holes will pull us at both of them. It might get a little stretchy, but if it's for a second, it would pull us right through. Then we just repeat the cycle again?" She looks at me for validation.

"Yeah, because time's a circle, remember? Let's just hope we start out with a really big one," I say, happy about being right for the first time. *This might just work.*

"So does anyone know how to make a black hole?"

Ouch, hadn't thought of that one.

OLIVIA THOMPSON

This was starting to get out of hand. What if we couldn't make a black hole in time? What if we couldn't make one at all? If that's the case, I wish I could see everyone, one last time—

"Seriously, stop complaining, Olivia, we're all scared enough without your little worries to make it worse," says Timmy in a small voice full of annoyance and a hint of fear.

I close my mouth even tighter. Had I really just said that out loud? I could have sworn that I was just thinking it.

"Oh, um, I'm sorry. That was my inside voice talking I guess," I say, trying to laugh it off.

"Umm, Timmy, Olivia didn't say anything," said Jessica, confused.

"Yes, she did. She said that this was getting too complicated, and she thought we couldn't make one and was like 'I wish I could've said my good-bye's' blah, blah, blah!" he says in a very bad imitation of me.

"But I didn't hear anything, and I was sitting right next to her," says Henry protectively.

"Yeah, I didn't hear anything either."

"Me neither."

"Nope, not over here," says people from around the room.

"Um, guys?" I begin trying to think how to say the impossible and make it sound plausible. "I think Timmy can read minds." That earns me a lot of confused looks from everyone. "I was thinking those very things, and Timmy was the only one who could hear them. Doesn't that sound some kind of an alarm bell?"

"Sure, but thinking you said something is one thing, being a mind reader is another," said Jessica, not quite believing.

"Then let's make a test. I will write something on my hand with the pen I keep in my boot," I say as I pull out the pen. "Timmy will be facing the other wall, and when I finish writing it, he will guess what's on my hand," I say, excited and worried.

"Okay, that sounds good," says Timmy, and he turns away from me.

As clear as I can, I write "*double-sided*" on my hand. "Okay, guess," I say and concentrate on the word as hard as I can.

"Double-sided," he says instantly.

Everyone looks at me for validation. I turn my hand for them to see, and everyone gasps. Exactly what I had written.

"Well, that can't be a coincidence. But does it only work on Olivia?" asks Henry, and for the next ten minutes, everyone takes turns, from different distances and harder words, every time within an instant.

"Okay, so if he has a special power, does everyone? Like, I mean, is that why Eric picked us because we have undiscovered powers?" I asked, hoping I had some awesome kick-butt power too. And now that I think about it, no wonder I could never hide anything from him, because he could read my mind, literally! And of course in the normal world where black holes and super powers aren't exactly normal, we never would've guessed! And this morning! When I was thinking how nice he looked, I didn't accidentally say it out loud! He was reading my mind! Gosh, that was mortifying all by itself.

So what felt like days, we checked people for every superpower we had ever read or thought about, and as it turned out, everyone had a power, all of which had definitely stumbled upon it before this. Except for one person named Bay, she doesn't have one...

The whiteboard was still here; and it had an Expo pen and eraser in the tray, so I decided to get organized. I made a list of everything we knew and drew a table of the person, their name, and the power they have, and it looked something like this:

What we know:

- Time is a circle
- Circles makes thread
- Each thread is a universe
- Thread makes fabric
- Fabric is in bad shape
- The end of the world is in twelve days and counting

- The end is the sun exploding into a super nova making a black hole
- We need to make a black hole and send it to destroy the other black hole
- Fabric gone
- New start

# of people	Persons name	Age	Power
1	Chelsey	15 yrs	Super speed
2	Valery	14yrs	Healing
3	Andrew	13 yrs	Super human reflexes
4	Adam	12yrs	Transportation
5	Lilia	12yrs	Imitation
6	Timmy	13yrs	Telepathic/ see through walls
7	Olivia	10yrs	Lie detector
8	Henry	13yrs	Can tell future (within a week)
9	Jessica	13yrs	Mind control
10	Stan	22yrs	Freeze/heat things
11	Josh	15yrs	Force field
12	Bay	13yrs	Unknown

BAY TINE

The first thing that I thought when I woke up in that room, strapped to a chair next to Andrew was *You had to ask for action, Andrew!* But that wasn't fair; obviously it wasn't his fault, which in a way made me feel like it was my fault, and really, it felt good to have him here, even if he was strapped to a chair. Shaking off my guilt, I try to pay attention, but after we found out that Timmy and everyone else had powers, that just about tipped the scale on my calm sanity.

Each power seemed important, and I totally saw Andrew's coming, like right before the accident, no way someone normal could've reacted that fast. Which made me feel even guiltier since he seemed to be having so much fun working on his awesome superpower. But I couldn't focus on them, all I could think about was my power…nothing. It still feels wrong. Some people say that we just haven't found it yet, others say that we can't tell in this room, or that I might not have one. But something was wrong with that last one. Why would I be the only one without a power? Eric said he chose everyone for a reason. *My reason can't be that I'm pretty*, I think bitterly. It feels like something's missing, something important...but what?

Oh how much I yearned to be back in the car on the road with Andrew, not worrying about doomsday. The good thing is that all the worry is distracting from my parents; the little boo-boo though is that we have to *save the whole world*! No, not anything like "donate three dollars to help plant trees in the rain forest" or "Don't litter! Keep it green!" No, we get save the whole freaking world, then if you survive, you might have some more time before it blows up again!

Even though I was upset, and even though the news was pretty bizarre, everyone seemed to believe it, like no one in this whole place for one second thought this was some kind of joke, prank, whatever; and to be honest, as much as I wanted this to all be a hoax, I believed it too.

Well, I can't just pout in a corner this whole time, and no way am I going to let Jessica take the entire leadership role. Even if I don't have a power, I can still help lead.

"Okay, so if we were picked for a reason, what better reason than the fact that we have superpowers? But now we need a plan, if we were taken April 5, then I am to presume that doomsday is on Tuesday the 17th. So we need to get moving on the world saving," I say, silencing the mindless chatter of the other kids.

"Yeah, I've been thinking about it a lot, and I was trying to figure out which Tuesday we're supposed to be at," says Henry.

"Um, the only Tuesday I can remember being called *doomsday* is the 17. You know five plus twelve equals seventeen?" I say, irritation taking over.

"No, I mean like *which* one, like if I were to go to New York, that's like four hours ahead of the west coast, so they would reach it at a different time as us, and if we were in Africa, that's almost a whole day's difference. So which one is on the countdown?" he says. The room erupts into a fit of discussions on the topic.

"Wouldn't it be in Greenwich? That's like the standard clock 'cause it's right on the 0,0 degree mark. It's the perfect point to make a black hole and hurl it at the sun if you think about it," says Timmy.

"No, no, we should do it at the astronomical clock in Colorado. It has the time and shows where the sun will be," a kid named Adam remarked.

"Um...Wouldn't it be the Tuesday that comes first?" asks Olivia quietly.

"It could or it couldn't...We don't know, but we need some more clues," I say, that of course is when the room erupts into another loud conversation.

"Quiet! You all have great points, but why don't we go to them all? That way if we're wrong, we still have a backup," I say, silencing the crowd.

"She's right. We have Adam who can transport us to whichever clock is the right one," says Henry, taking my back.

"So here is the short plan, half of us goes to the astronomical clock in Colorado, half will go to Greenwich. We will have Timmy to help us communicate. When doomsday comes, Josh will put his force field around earth. You know, just so there isn't a chance of us turning to noodles, and it will keep our atmosphere in the green. Then all we have to do is make a black hole and have someone else push us in-between without killing us, and time will build on itself," I say, speaking more sense than I thought was possible.

"Well, that's great but now I was thinking…you know how the sun is so far away?" Nods go around the room. "Well, is the sun going to blow up at twelve 'cause then it wouldn't even be here until eight minutes after, which is the time it takes for light to travel to earth, but if it were to blow up at eleven fifty-two, then it would be here around twelve o'clock, so which one?" says Henry *know-it-all*! I almost yelled out, but he did have a point.

"Why don't you find out," I start to ask, "since you can see the future?"

This idea looked like it made Henry nervous, but he agreed.

"Okay, hate to burst your guy's bubble here. But I am certain that I know which Thursday it will happen on," says Lilia.

OLIVIA THOMPSON

"Well, feel free to share it," Jessica bites out, obviously upset with Lilies sureness.

"Well, what's the magic word then?" she responds, happily toying with Jessica.

"Come on! This isn't all fun and games!" says Adam coldly.

"*Oh come on! You could use a little fun!*" says Lilia, imitating Adam perfectly; Adam on the other hand looked at her murderously. What was that about?

"Anyway, like I was saying…the Eric dude already gave us the answer," she said nonchalantly.

"And how do you know that?" I ask, interested now.

"Well, remember when he was talking about Roanoke?" she asks the group, nods go around, and she continues with, "Well, what did he tell us?"

"Nothing really, just how his many greats grandpa bought us some time," says Adam not catching on, but I was.

"Exactly, he saved the world from the beginning of the end…from Roanoke! That's where it will take place!" I say enthusiastically.

"That's great, but do you guys know the time?" asks Adam, still seeming pissed off at Lilia from that previous remark

"Well, duh," replies Lilia.

"Okay then, do I have to say please?" replies Adam bitterly.

"Well, it would help," says Lilia smiling. "But I will tell you guys anyway," she says happily.

"So…then what?" I ask, eager as ever.

"Well, you know how in numerology Croatoan is equal to twelve thousand?" she replies with a question. Nods go around the room; all eyes were on her. "Well, Croatoan wasn't the only thing written on a tree. The word 'CRO' was on another tree nearby." She pauses for emphasis. "Now, I'm not exactly an expert at this numerology stuff, but the numbers would be three, eight, six," she says, waiting for this to sink in.

"So what do we do? Multiply, add, subtract?" asks Timmy, dumbfounded.

"Well, now this is still kind of in the thinking zone here, but if you multiply them, you get one hundred forty-four," she says, her brow furrowed as if she were checking her answer in her head.

"So? What's the point? I mean, one hundred twenty isn't exactly a time, is it?" asks Timmy.

"Well, that's what I was thinking, so I was experimenting and thought that the square root of one hundred forty-four is twelve," she says as if she were explaining a math equation to a teacher.

"Okay, so?" says Timmy, confused again.

"That's when I remembered the whole thing about how it takes eight minutes for the sun's light to travel. I think the black hole will reach us by 12 pm April 17th," she finished, smiling at her achievement.

"Okay, so if that's true, we would have to create our black hole around 11:52?" Timmy states, looking around for any objections.

"Okay, so on Thursday at about 11:52 we will make a black hole, go through it, and be done, right?" asked the man named Stan. He had kept relatively to himself the whole time, but now that our plan was unfolding even he couldn't resist.

"So how do we get out of this metal box?" I say, becoming more aware of where we were.

That's when Timmy let out a scream; it was a bloodcurdling scream that would've brought giants to their knees. Without thinking, I run to Timmy and catch him right before he passes out; I gently lay him down and check his breathing and pulse. It's normal.

"What happened?" I asked to no one in particular; I was too distressed to think clearly. Everyone just shakes their heads.

"Did he see something on the other side of the wall?" Henry asked. That made me nervous since he can see through walls—Which we only tried on chairs. Wow, we are really stupid, huh?—and he can turn it on and off , as well as focus on depth. *I really should've done this earlier*, I think, burdened with regret.

"Well, let's give him someone's water bottle and see if he comes to," I say, trying my best to recall everything Timmy had taught me—since he was a little preoccupied—but alas, no one had any provisions, so I resort to the thing I do best.

"Timmy! Wake up, now!" I yell over and over again.

But still he didn't wake up right away. I start to shake his shoulders and am still yelling his name when his eyes flutter open, but no "Oh you saved me thank you!" or "How long was I out?" He opens his eyes and gives me his right hook, then he screams again and punches me in the nose; I felt the warm blood sliding down my face and could taste the salty, thick syrup; *I'm going to be sick*, I thought, but I had to focus.

"Timmy, it's okay, we won't hurt you," I say calmly.

And of course, it the perfect time for Stan to add, "Yeah, nice punch by the way."

I glared at him with something I hoped would send as "*one more word and I won't be the only one with a broken nose!*" I think it worked too because he closed his mouth so fast his teeth made a loud clicking sound. I look back at Timmy; his eyes are closed, and he is breathing slowly.

"Timmy, what happened, what did you see?" I asked cautiously, not wanting another beating.

"I…I…It's dark outside, like we aren't on earth but somewhere else, then I saw it, it was terrible it was so…so…" He started stuttering, but I wasn't paying attention. Were we in space? What did he see that was so terrible?

"Timmy, what did you see that was so bad?" I ask in a soft whisper.

"I saw it! The sun! At least that's what it looked like, it looked almost possessed. It was dark and had a dark crust, then out of nowhere it started cracking! Like it was exploding! Now everything after is kind of fuzzy," he says, sounding like an insane person trying to convince someone that his dog can talk.

"Timmy, are we in space?" I ask nervously.

He looks at me and says yes.

"Henry? Has your future power shown this to you?" I ask accusingly. Was he keeping things from us?

Henry shakes his head violently. "No, I can only see it if I concentrate on the future."

"Well, concentrate now! What do you see?" I asked full of rage; Henry closes his eyes, then his bottom lip starts to quiver and then he starts to whimper quietly. *Uh-oh.*

"Henry, what is it? What do you see?" I asked, impatience, hiding my nervousness.

"Everything he said, it's not the future or the present…'cause from what it looks like, it's gotten a whole lot worse," he said, stuttering slightly. Still that managed to silence everyone. It felt as if the whole room was holding its breath.

"So we're the last ones? It's over?" asks Jessica with a strain to her voice.

"No, we all go remember? 'Cause everything will stop," says Lilia with a bored expression, but I could tell she was scared too.

"We still have time, but not much, it's the sixteenth—," says Henry before Chelsey interrupts him.

"Wait, we've been here for nearly eleven days!" asks Chelsey in her high shrill voice of hers.

"Yes, but since we're in space we—"

"We're in SPACE? How did we even get up here!?!?!" she says in an even higher-pitched voice, easily reaching a high C; I ached to scream at her to shut up, but starting a fight on the day before doomsday didn't appeal to me at the moment.

"Well, think about it. The police aren't just looking for one person, but twelve, and believe me, if we weren't in this... high security box, Lilia probably would've found a way to escape and be home right about now. And if the fabric of time can go from nonexistent to a black hole, I think a couple of highly advanced robots working for NASA can get us up here," explains Adam with reasonable logic.

"Whatever. What time is it now? How much time do we have?" I asked, trying to move the conversation along. "And how long will it take to get to earth?" I ask, realizing we could be too late; *this thing could end before it even started*, I think sadly.

"I don't know. Frankly, I don't know how we're going to move this prison in the first place," he said sullenly. *Crap, hadn't thought of that.*

BAY TINE

"Well, Adam has only transported within this place. He might be able to go farther when he's not in a spaceship... or whatever this thing is, so…can Jessica move other things? Like inanimate objects as well as people's minds and stuff?" asks Josh hopefully.

That only makes Henry shudder; I guess that would make a lot of people shudder, but he replies, "We have only tested it on people. She can make them say or do anything she wants, but we haven't tried it out on machines yet."

Everybody knew this, but she responds with "So let's try!" She says this a bit overenthusiastic. I look over at her, and her eyes are closed lightly, slightly fluttering; her hand rotated as if she were pulling the throttle on a motor, and with that, the entire room shakes and quivers, causing everyone to fall to the ground. *She did it!* I think, *hopefully*. Jessica's feet are planted firmly on the ground; I hear what sounds like gears shifting. *Yes!* Then in an instant, as quickly as it had started, nothing; no more ground-shaking gear shifting, anything, what? I look over at Jessica who lay on the floor covered in a thin layer of sweat; her body was contorting every which way. What was happening?

"She's having a seizure!" says Chelsey, again in her shrill voice.

"What do we do?" asks Adam.

For some reason, I found myself asking to know the answer; in my mind, I kept repeating, *What do I do?* Over and over, almost like a chant, soon it felt as though my thoughts were hollow except for those four words; everything else seems to blur behind me as if it were passing through thick syrup.

Then like a blender was mixing my brain into slush, I get a splintering pain behind my eyes. I shut them to stop the tears, and just like that, pictures were swirling through my head behind my eyes and crashing on the inside of my skull as if trying to break free. I was vaguely aware of my mouth moving, but afterwards, everything went dark—no more headache, no pictures, just a whole lot of nothing.

Slowly the blackness retreated from my eyes, and I woke to the whole room's eyes on me. *What happened?* I think. My thoughts were disoriented, my head was swirling, but it no longer felt like my head was being crushed to pieces. Again as I look around, the people's expressions vary from disbelief to concern. Not understanding, I ask, "Whatttappened? I…I feewoozy," I ask drunkenly, slurring my words together.

"What happened?" I try again with more success.

"You saved me," says a voice behind me; I turn around slowly—completely aware of a head-splitting headache coming on—to find Jessica staring at me wide-eyed.

"I…I saved you?" I ask in disbelief.

"Well, that's what everyone has told me," she replies, not looking me in the eyes and with uncertainty in her voice while her hands were curled into fists at her sides.

"Well, can someone please tell me what I've done?" I ask, anger replacing my wooziness.

"You said this weird chant thing…and the when you blacked out, Jessica got up like nothing had happened," says Andrew.

"Well, what did I say?" I asked, interested now. *Could this be my power?*

"Well, you said something like…stamatísei, típota perissótero," says Lilia, matching my voice perfectly.

"What the heck does that mean?" I ask thunderstruck. How did I say that?

"Well, it means, *stop no more* in Greek," says Lilia again.

"Wait, how do you know?" I ask as the thought passed my mind.

"Well, when I heard you say it, I knew right away, but since I can imitate people, I guess I also know like a million languages too. I don't know, it just happened," she says without much certainty.

"Okay, so does this mean I have a power?" I ask, praying silently.

"Well, I guess, but what is it?" asked Henry that left me with a bad feeling.

"Well, we will find it. We just need some tests," says Andrew confidently.

"Yeah, okay then," I say with some reserve. The last time I did it, I felt like I was going to die…Could it kill me? Will it be like that every time? Questions like these flowed through my head, making my previous worries seem like a day at the park.

"So maybe you have the power to create your own power," says Timmy helpfully. "That's always been my first power of choice."

"Or it could just be a coincidence," said Stan grumpily.

"Or it could be that you can heal by mind control," says Andrew through gritted teeth; he was giving Stan a "*if you mess with her, you mess with me*" kind of look. He held this gaze for what seemed like hours till finally he turned to me and gave me one of his beautiful smiles.

From that moment, with everything in my power, I wanted to thank Andrew for always being there; I just couldn't find the right words. That's when I felt the all too familiar headache.

It was less painful, but it still brought me to my knees not in control of my own thoughts. I see images—all the times Andrew was there for me. All my thoughts were wrapped into those pictures. If it weren't so painful, I would've smiled. *If only I could show him.*

Soon enough, the headache turned into a tsunami in my head, and all the images started to glow in my mind to a point where they burn my eyes, unaware that tears were streaking my face and that I was clutching myself tightly in odd, twitchy motions; my legs crumble under my weight, and I feel myself convulsing.

"She's going into a seizure!" exclaimed Andrew as he kneels down beside me, just then I have the strange urge to hold his hand—and no, not the teenage hormonal kind; my hand still shaking, my body racking and shivering, I hold out my hand. Knowingly, he grasps it, watching my face with a concerned look in his eyes.

Black starts to crowd out my vision, then, the images, all of them, start to pass through me; everything I've always wanted to tell him, then, in a blink, they're gone. Nothing. I couldn't even remember them. *No!* I felt like screaming. They were so beautiful! They made me feel so warm, so safe.

As quickly as it came, it went away faster. My headache was substituted with an odd tingly sensation that went from my toes to the ends of my fingertips and all the way up to the tippy top of my head. I felt so warm and happy that I was only partially aware of myself smiling the biggest grin the world has yet to see.

"Bay," says Andrew, looking shell-shocked.

"Huh?" I say gleefully.

"I understand," said Andrew sullenly.

"What?" I ask mystified,

"Those pictures, they…they…I understand," he said again, this time smiling uncontrollably.

"Wait…what happened?" I ask, aware of everyone's eyes on me.

"Well, you said, 'May my pictures tell a thousand words' in Greek, had a second seizure, and are now smiling like a babbling idiot," said Lilia, happily changing her voice to meet mine, and somehow finding a way to humiliate me in front of the rest of the group

"Okay, so this is definitely a power," I say almost sorrowfully.

"Well, it's actually pretty cool. I think you can say spells," says Timmy again, cheering me up even though we were basically complete strangers.

"Yeah, but it hurts," I say, remembering the unspeakable pain.

"Well...maybe because you are remembering them from like your great, great, great, great, great—"

"WE GET IT!" Olivia interrupts.

"But like I was saying, maybe it's like deep inside you, and it's like trying to surface," he finishes.

"Yeah, and maybe it only knows how to do it through headaches," adds Josh, joining the conversation.

"So maybe all you have to do is find a way to channel it...you know, without having a seizure," says Adam.

"No, this doesn't make sense. Why would we all have normal super powers, then she has some crazy spell casting witch thing?" asks Valery.

"Well, maybe it's not really her power, maybe that's just a reflex, you know there are Greek and Latin roots in everything. I'm surprised I can't speak them myself," says Henry.

"Yeah, you could have such a powerful super power that subconsciously that's the only way you know how to activate it. I bet if you keep using it, it will come more naturally to you," says Jessica.

"Yeah...but we don't have time. We have to get to earth," I say, remembering our dilemma.

"Bay, you know I would never ask this unless it was really important...but do you think you can try to take us back?" asked Andrew. It looked like it pained him to say it, but it was true, I was the only one the power to do it.

"Well, you know what they say...the bigger it is, the harder it falls," I say under my breath; this only worries everyone else.

"Yo, um, princess...try to make sure it doesn't fall 'cause I would prefer not to look like roadkill when we land," says Josh.

Okay, personality check? "Sure, will do!" I say with an unrealistic smile that basically beamed sarcasm.

"That's great," he replied, partially taken aback by my chucky smile.

"Okay, hate to rush your little moment and all, but we kind of have a world to save here," comments Lilia. Okay, I could do this...right?

STAN PRICE

Okay, and I thought being in a jail cell was bad, but after being locked in a space shuttle with a bunch of kids with freaking superpowers was worse. And to add to this, some dead guy somehow convinced us we have to save the world…universe…time…or whatever he called it. Now don't get me wrong, the five minutes of fame was pretty nice; I still feel bad about torching Josh's eye brows though, and for the record, that was a complete accident. Thank god that Valery has healing powers, which include new eyebrow hair growth.

After a while, I forget about E. J. by thinking that he's back at home trying to figure out what happened that night…or he's in jail. Eric didn't exactly specify what happened to those at home, but we have a world to save, and friends weren't on the agenda I guess.

Now, to me it felt like this whole plan was built on what-ifs and theories. Like sure, Croatoan may equal twelve thousand in numerology, but why would it mean we have gone a full circle that many times? Why can't it mean that's the number of species that have healing qualities to humans? I don't know, but this whole "save the world" thing wasn't sitting well with me. But since everyone else was having a good time being little superheroes, I decided to keep my mouth shut.

Okay, I would never say this out loud, but Bay really was starting to freak me out. Like not only does she have some sort of super-super power, she's had two seizures within twenty minutes, and now she's going to fly a space shuttle. *Well, that's not unnerving at all!*

"Okay, hold on to your hats, everyone!" Bay says with a determined look. *This is it*, I thought as she goes into her typical creepy convulsing; her legs buckle, and she goes into another fit of spasms. If I wasn't so freaked out, I probably would've done something…Well, I probably wouldn't either way since she was doing all this on purpose, but it's the thought that counts, right?

After what seems like five minutes of being seized with spasms, she lets out something that sounds like a howl then after that she practically screams "Kinoúntai, sti̱ Gi̱ telikó proorismó mas!" over and over again.

"What does that mean?" asked Andrew, concern etched into every inch of his face.

I felt bad for him. It was so obvious that he was close to her, and she obviously meant a lot to him, and if I couldn't look at her without getting the shivers, well, it probably sucked ten times worse for him, but was I going to do anything? Nope. Sometimes it's best to stay out of other people's lives. But the fact is there was nothing really to say. She was having her little "moment," and when it was over hopefully we would be on earth and not human pancakes.

"Um, it's something like…move to earth our final destination," replies Lilia. Okay, creepy? Yes. Something about that last part, "*our final destination*," gave me the heebie-jeebies.

All of a sudden, the ship lurched in a direction. Did I know what it was? No, because apparently, they forgot to add a window in this metal prison-space shuttle-whatchamacallit. But that lurch led to another and another till it was a steady rhythm to a point where it felt as though we weren't even moving at all.

Bay still twitching on the ground, but her ear-piercing screams had died out. Thankfully. It felt like somehow we could do it. I mean, save the world, like what's there to lose? It's an all or nothing at this point. We had to try; even if their little theories turn out wrong, at least we can say we tried. But now wasn't a time to think of what happens if we fail or succeed.

"Bay...Bay, you did it! Are you okay?" asks Andrew, and again, I come back to earth,—metaphorically speaking of course—and look at Bay. She looked so weak and fragile, sitting up with Andrew at her side; the thought crossed my mind that maybe she could die using this power too often. By the looks of it, the way she put her hand up to her brow, still probably dizzy and nauseous from her last spell-thing proved my point; at least I thought it did, but I didn't want to worry anyone...yet.

"Yeah, I'm fine...Are we there yet?" she asked softly through a smile that I couldn't tell was forced or authentic.

"Well, if we're here, we didn't go splat," says Timmy. Did he read my mind? A shiver passed through me reminding me of the capabilities these kids have. *It's okay, Stan, just watch what you think. You'll be fine*, said a voice in my head, but it wasn't my voice; I looked at Timmy and meet his gaze. Timmy smiled a devilish smile and turns his attention back to Bay. *Remind me to kill that kid, would you?* I think to myself extra hard to make certain he could hear me.

"So how do we get out?" asks Timmy, avoiding my eyes.

"Well, let's just make sure we're on earth first," I say, thinking of how it would be really bad if we busted out the walls, and we ended up still being in space...*Wait, don't think!* I remind myself, stealing a look at Timmy; never thought I would say or think that.

"Timmy?" implies Henry, and just like that, Timmy gives a nod. *My turn*, I think happily.

Now my power was kind of weird because I could either freeze or burn things just by thinking about it, or my hands could explode with lava or snow or whatever; well, this was a job for the lava. Slowly I draw a circle with my awesome lava hands, and the whole things just melts off.

"Air!" says someone.

"Land!" says another.

"WATER!" screams another one as we all realize that we were floating, and the hole I made is letting in water faster than I would like to admit.

"Everyone out!" I yell as everyone pushes to get out before the whole thing goes down under, not even thinking I could just freeze the water.

"Hey, Adam, can you get us to land?" asks Lilia, treading water.

"Yeah, but not on land, if anyone saw me and you guys just...appear, we'll be science experiments, that, and I don't know where we would land. We could all land on top of some kids buried in the sand for all I—"

"Yeah, yeah, we get it, just get us out of here," Lilia replies, spitting out sea water.

"Okay, okay, everyone grab each other's hands. Don't want anyone to get left behind," he says as we just pop into a new place. We're right on the coast near a beach.

"Nice job," says Lilia, already swimming in.

VALERY JACKSON

This whole experience has been more than traumatic, but just popping ashore on a beach in Virginia is a little weird. I don't know about everyone else, but this all seems too easy. But I go along with it.

So we're trying to find a map when we come to a small beach shack.

"Um…hello?" asks Josh, peering in, a man appears in front of us and smiles.

"What can I do for you?" he asks properly.

"Um…what's the time? Oh, and do you have a map we can use?" Josh asks, not really looking him in the eyes.

"Well, it looks like it's five minutes to nine, and do you want a tour guide or just one of the area?" he asks kindly.

"Can we get one that shows all of Virginia…and of North Carolina?" asks Josh with a shy smile.

"Um…you might just be in luck. Let me look." He disappears into the shack and returns with a folded piece of paper. "Here it is!" he says and hands us the map.

"Thanks…How much?" asks Josh, looking at the map.

"It's free, have fun," he says happily.

"Yeah, okay, kooky head," replies Lilia after he leaves. Adam nudges her, trying to quiet her, only to get a clod glare in return.

"Let's go," says Timmy, seeming antsy, and I don't blame him; we don't have a lot of time to waste here.

"Wait, I thought Roanoke was in Virginia, that's why they named the girl Virginia," says Chelsey. I couldn't help but roll my eyes.

"No, the lost colony would be around modern-day North Carolina," I say.

"Okay, well, I say we teleport close by somewhere in the woods right by the Virginia Dare memorial bridge, then we can see where to go from then 'cause otherwise we won't have enough time to get there," says Andrew, finally rejoining the conversation.

"Yeah, that sounds good," replies Adam, but his face was white as a sheet.

"Okay, see here?" Stan points to a green area about only a couple miles away from the Roanoke site. "Adam, can you get us this far?" he asks.

"Um…I think so," he replies, not so reassuringly.

"Okay then, let's get this over with," says Chelsey in her high-pitched voice.

"Grab hands, everyone!" Adam says, and just like that, we're in the woods. Wow, that'll never get old.

"Which way is the road?" asks Bay, turning in a circle.

"That way." Adam points in a direction. "Here, hold on, and I'll get us closer," he says, and we're there.

"Hey…is that a…grocery store?" asks Bay, rubbing her stomach lightly; I hear my own stomach growl, but we had no time to lose so I knew that wouldn't be an option.

"Great!" exclaims Lilia. "We can steal a couple of cars so we won't have to walk it," she says happily, probably dreaming of comfy seats instead of the cold metal ones in the space shuttle thing.

"I have to agree with Lilia on this one. It would save us a lot of time," says Henry; nods go around the group. O*kay, stealing cars it is*, I think to myself. And together still damp from the ocean, we walk over to the grocery store looking through all the cars.

"Here, this one will work," says Stan, looking at a minivan. "It'll seat six comfortably, and the less amount of cars we have to steal, the better," says Stan, talking more sense than anyone here. "That, and this one has a GPS, so you guys can take the map," he says, handing Josh the map.

"Okay, so, Stan, you can drive and why don't you take the younger kids like"—I look around—"Timmy, Olivia, Henry, Jessica, and Lilia?" I say. "You know, since you're the only one who actually has a driver's license," I continue.

"Um…if you haven't forgotten, I'm wanted by the law, so it really won't matter in the end if I have a driver's license or not," he says kind of bitterly.

"Well, can you take them?" I ask.

"Yeah, sure…Get in, kids," he says. "It'll only take me a minute to hot-wire this bad boy," he says as they all load up.

"Okay, Chelsey, you know how to drive…right?" I ask.

"Yeah, tomorrow was the day I was supposed to take my driver's test. I'm the best driver in all of Florida," she says in a normal voice for once.

"Okay then, the rest of us will be together," says Josh as he stalks past us looking for another car to steal.

"Hey, how about this one?" asks Chelsey, pointing to another minivan almost identical to the other one, but this one was black, not tan. "It even has the keys in them," she says, opening the door, and we're off.

So in the car Chelsey has the radio on and is singing along, which she isn't that bad at actually. Adam was looking out the window beside me. Bay and Andrew are playing I-Spy quietly in the back, and Josh was looking at the map sitting shotgun. All was good, and for the first time since we got here, I've actually had something that resembles fun. Not that crashing to earth in a spaceship, transporting more than once from the ocean to the shore and to the woods, and after all that, stealing a car and driving to where Roanoke was, and on top of that, the pressure of saving the universe isn't fun...actually, I lied. It's terrifying. But that's not really the point.

We've been driving for a good five minutes, so all anxiety to stealing the car has numbed itself out of mind. Well, at least till we see a police car.

"Crap, it's the cops!" exclaims Bay from the back.

"No freaking way. I would have never known that," replies Adam, turning to stare at the flashing headlights.

"Hey, when have you started sounding like Lilia?" Bay says. I giggle.

"Come on, guys, this isn't the problem we should be bickering about," says Josh, turning around in his seat to stare at the two.

"Whatever," replies Adam.

"Sure, fine," Bay comments.

"Good. Now, Chelsey, can you lose them?" Josh asks, keeping a cool, even tone.

"Well, I would, but the car's not…working," she says with wide eyes. Josh's eyes go wide too, just now noticing how the car is stopped in the middle of the road.

"What!" he exclaims. "What's wrong? Why won't it go!" he says right as the police officers tell us to get out of the car, and they have guns.

"You guys, we can't get caught," says Andrew in a loud whisper. "If they catch us, we are either going to jail or going back to wherever we came from," he says, his voice wavering a little.

"It'll be fine, guys. We were made for this," I say reassuringly as the cops are holding guns to the windows. They say for us to get out, and what choice do we have?

"Yeah," replies Adam in a mild tone, not really focusing on us. "You guys! When you get out of the car, hold on to it!" he says, sounding crucial. They tell us to get out of the car again, which leaves us no choice.

"Umm…Is there a problem officer?" asks Chelsey in an even voice.

"You stole one of our bait cars. You're under arrest for auto theft," says a cop. "Put your hands behind your head, and step away from the vehicle," he continues.

"You guys, now!" shouts Adam. I put my hand on the car, and just like that, we're off to the side of the road, but there was no police cars. Actually, there weren't any cars at all really.

"Everyone okay?" Adam shouts from the other side of the minivan.

"Yeah, I'm fine," says Chelsey.

"Same here," replies Andrew.

"Me too," comments Josh.

"Me three," says Bay.

"Yep," I say when it's my turn.

"Good, everyone's here," replies Adam with a sigh of relief. I couldn't even begin to imagine what would happen if one of us had been left there. I shudder, then open the car door.

"We can't," says Josh, finishing my nonexistent thought.

"But why?" I whine.

"Because it's a bait car. They can shut these things down from anywhere and can track us too," replies Josh.

"At least we're all here…Um, where is here?" asks Chelsey.

"We are less than a half mile away from the site. We can walk it," says Josh, looking at the map.

"Adam, you're a genius!" exclaims Bay, happily giving him a hug; Adam looks uncomfortable though, and so does Andrew.

"Okay then. We'll get there and wait for the others," I say, not including the "*if they make it in time*" part.

LILIA RIDER

"Shut up!" I scream. I was not in the mood for bickering, and let me tell you, Olivia and Timmy were totally full of it.

"Well, he started it!" she complains.

"No, you did!" he quips.

"Shut up, both of you! Do you think I care? Shut up and look out the window or something," I say, feeling my blood boil.

"Come on now, Lilia. Can you be any more cruel?" asks Stan from the wheel.

"Oh yeah, watch me," I begin happily. "Ahem, *I hate you! No, I hate you! I hate you more! No, I hate you more! I hate puppies! Well I hate kittens!*" I say, changing my voice from Olivia to Timmy.

"That's enough from you unless you want me to torch your eyebrows," says Stan menacingly, but I don't show fear or mercy.

"*Yeah, I'm some mean police dude and will burn off the eyebrows of innocent children*," I say in his voice; he turns around and gives me a steely look, but he doesn't do any harm to my eyebrows.

"*Are you seriously going to take that?*" I say, mimicking Henry.

"Shut up, Henry, no one asked you," he says bitterly and everyone, except for Henry and Stan, snicker quietly.

"What's so funny!" he complains angrily, only fueling our laughter.

"*Never mind*," I say in Timmy's voice, and he gives me a hard glare but doesn't comment.

"Okay, whatever," replies Stan grumpily, and for the next five seconds, there is perfect silence.

"Stop pushing my seat!"

"I'm not!"

"Yes, you are!"

"Shut up, or I'll shut you up for you!" I yell at them seething, and finally there is silence.

One hour later...

"Are we there yet?" asks Henry.

"No," replies Stan.

"When will we get there anyway?" Olivia asks.

"Well, there's a lot of traffic on the bridge. Everybody's probably going to the airport. So maybe half an hour, forty-five minutes?" says Stan, rechecking the GPS.

"Thank god!" I say so happy I only have half an hour left of listening to these aggravating kids! The saddest thing of all being I'm the second youngest in the group.

"Hey, Timmy, how are the other kids doing?" I ask, trying not to think about Adam, yet Timmy smiles knowingly and closes his eyes.

"Well, from the looks of it, they're almost there, but they're walking," he says after a minute of concentrating;

he's really getting good at that since they're so far away and all.

"Thanks, means a lot when it comes from you," says Timmy with a smile, and I nearly curse in my head, then I scold myself about how I can't think anymore with a mind reader sitting next to me. Do you know how hard that is to basically shut off your thoughts? Well, it's freaking hard. Everyone gives us curious look, but I wave it off and look out the window scowling.

"Hey, guys, how do you feel about walking?" asks Stan about twenty minutes later.

"Actually, I hate walking, and I feel that walking is a waste of time, like really, if you really want a work out, try talking to these two," I say, pointing to Timmy and Olivia, "because it takes a really strong mind to keep cool in their chaos. And if you really want to go somewhere, take a bus, a bike, at least a slow jog, like really, walking?"

"Thanks for your opinion, but I wasn't really asking. We're going to be walking any minute," he says, looking at me with stern eyes.

"And why is that old wise one?" I ask, knives shooting off my tongue.

"Well, we're running out of gas," he says angrily right as the engine sputters.

"No! No, no, no!" yells Olivia, and right then, I felt like doing the same.

"Well, looks like we're walking it," says Stan under his breath.

"Wait," says Jessica, eyes closed in concentration.

"Jessica, what are you doing?" asks Henry confused, just then a car makes a U-turn and drives up right beside us; actually, it was a badass Hummer limo that looked seriously pimped. "Jessica," says Henry cautiously.

"Shut up, Henry," Timmy says. He must be reading her mind, I think. All of the sudden, a couple get out.

"Oh no, we can't do this!" exclaims Olivia.

"It's either this or walk," says Stan straight-faced.

"But they just got married! She's still in her dress! We can't just leave them here!" she yells hysterically.

"Olivia, there won't be a *here* if we can't get to Roanoke. If you really care, you'll know that this is the only way," says Stan gently.

"Fine, but we're kicking out the driver too," she says, still sniffling; no one asks the reason. There really wasn't any time.

"Don't forget the GPS," I warn Stan; he goes to the car and pulls it out.

"Got it," he says, putting it on the dashboard in the front. After we kick out the driver, we drive off at top speed—which is about ten miles an hour—with a full tank of gas, thankfully.

"Are we lost?" asks Timmy sleepily.

"No," replies Stan from the front.

"Are we close?" asks Jessica.

"Yes," he replies again.

"How long?" asks Henry.

"We'll be there by ten," says Stan dismissively; I look at the clock on the screen it read,

External temperature 58°
Interior temperature 78°
Monday, April 16
9:45 p.m.

I sigh with relief, only fifteen minutes! My eyes start to feel heavy, so I slide my seat belt off and lay on the floor, cushioning my head with my hands. I look around one last time to see that everyone but Jessica was asleep back here.

"Do you think we can do it?" she asks in a whisper.

"Well, what do we have to lose?" I say seriously. If we failed, it wouldn't really matter because everyone everywhere will be dead; we've won't exactly be missing out on much. But if we succeed, then we win, and everything will go back to normal. I don't want to call it a win-win necessarily because I still want to do so much before I have to die. It just feels so all-or-nothing kind of, even if I wanted to, I can't quite. I wish I could. But for once in my life, I can't ignore it by putting on earbuds or beating it up. And I think that was the scariest part, that something in the crazy messed-up universe, something is actually bigger than me, bigger than everyone.

For the first time since I woke up, I actually start to think about Mark. Was he really some voice-bot? I guess that explains all the weirdness back at school. But why would he say he would be "killed"? And from the sounds of it, he already knew bout the black hole. Was he simply malfunctioning? A glitch in the software? It seems hard to believe, but with no way to know for sure, it's the most comforting thought.

"Yeah, well, I guess you're sort of right," says Jessica, pondering over my answer.

"I think we will, and if we don't…Well, we'll go down in glory," I say, but I couldn't help adding, "or in flame." Jessica only seems sad. Now I'm not exactly the person to go to for advice and all, so I leave it at that. "I'm going to crash. Good night," I say.

"Good night," replies Jessica sleepily. I yawn once, twice, and then I'm out in a wonderful, dreamless sleep.

JOSH WILLIAMS

It didn't take long to get to Roanoke after Adam transported us within a mile of the place; although I basically had to carry Chelsey during the last stretch since she was whining so much about how her feet hurt and how she didn't have any shoes on. Chelsey might not be good at math or science or history or any other academic subject, but when it comes to getting what she wants, she would be passing with flying colors.

"What time is it?" asks Adam.

"Why are you asking us? We don't have a watch," I reply, irritated at the stupid question.

"Well, it's pretty dark. Where are the others? Timmy said they would be here a lot sooner," he quips.

"Well, we'll just have to wait," says Valery, obviously tired too.

"Hey, Adam, can you transport things that aren't within your touch?" asks Bay curiously; the bags under her eyes were so noticeable that I could still see them in the dim light.

"I don't know, haven't tried it," he replies, quietly averting his eyes to his feet.

"Well, try to get a big tent from a store, imagine you're walking into a store, and grabbing the biggest tent in the whole place," she says in a kind of storytelling voice.

"Ok…I'll try," he says, closing his eyes, his hands griping the sides of his shirt.

"You guys, just a thought, but let's step back," says Chelsey, and right as we step out of the way, the biggest tent I've ever seen.

"Holy—," I start.

"Cow," Valery finishes.

"Nice work, Adam. Are you okay? Do you feel like there's a limit to your powers?" asks Bay curiously, and I'm a bit taken aback by her sudden interest in Adam's powers, but I let it slide.

"Um, well, I don't feel tired, and I don't know if there's a limit. I definitely have to be thinking about it for me to be able to transport things not in my grasp. Other than that I guess we'll find out one way or another, right?" he answers nonchalantly, but I could tell he wasn't feeling his best.

"Yeah, I guess," says Bay, almost a little disappointed.

"Okay, well, if you can get the others here, a fire, and maybe some food and blankets, you'll be everyone's hero," says Andrew.

"Let's take this one at a time, shall we?" Adam replies, a little annoyed; his hands fumble at his sides.

"Yeah, sure, do you think you can get the others?" asks Andrew.

"Um, I'll try, but I might just have to get them individually," answers Adam.

"Okay, take your time," comments Bay reassuringly.

"Okay, I'll start with Lilia, 'cause she doesn't freak out as much as the others do," he says. I smile to myself, *Right, okay*, I think.

"Okay, here it goes," he says. A couple seconds go by, but nothing happens. "I'm going to try to bring the whole car. Watch out," he says. This worries me a bit, but we step back, and he closes his eyes again. And again we all hold our breath. Two seconds, three seconds, four—*poof!*—a huge black Hummer limo is within a fingernail's distance from hitting me. Bay and Olivia are screaming like a bunch of banshees. I don't blame them; I felt like wailing with them.

"Adam! Wrong car!" screams Valery, but looking through the car window, there is Stan looking petrified.

"No! It's them, see, here's Stan!" I yell to them so they wouldn't put it back.

"Hey, I can talk you know," says Stan, turning off the engine and opening the door.

"I know, but you looked a little…never mind. What happened?" I ask, curious at why *Just Married* was written on all the windows.

For the next hour, we swap stories about our journey over here while Stan starts the fire and Adam gets some food and blankets. Of course, the first ones to crash were Timmy, Olivia, and Henry; but for some reason, Lilia and Jessica also head in for the night fairly early.

"We should get some rest, we have to be at our strongest for tomorrow," says Valery.

"Yeah, I'm so tired I could sleep till the end of time," jokes Adam.

"Well, it's closer than you think," says Bay sleepily, but there is a harsh tone to her voice.

"Okay, I'll keep watch," offers Stan, but he looked beat from all the driving.

"No, I can, and if anything happens, I'll wake you up," I say. He doesn't even argue. He just nods his head while they all get inside the tent. I keep a blanket and sift through some of the kindling trying to keep the fire going.

It's really a gorgeous night; it's pitch-black, but the moon casts silvery shadows on the whole forest, and the stars are so vibrant, they almost seem like small flashlights shining down.

"Huh, I guess I found my clique," I say, smiling to myself. I wasn't scared; in fact, it was actually the opposite. Everyone here knew what we had to do, and it seemed simple enough, and like Eric said, the plan was flawless.

We are all different, yet one simple thing brings us all together. And even though the whole kidnapping thing was not cool, or him making such mean voice-bots, Eric Nova really did bring us all together.

Soon enough, I was counting the stars just to stay awake, fighting off sleepiness was like trying to swim with no arms or legs, and you could certainly bob for a while, just…not long enough.. Soon enough, I fell into a fitful sleep, and eventually, I was out so hard if you were to dump me into the ocean, I still wouldn't wake.

At first everything was black, no dream, no thoughts, then as if I'm awake, I'm standing at the Roanoke site; its daylight out, and it looks the same as before, but there's no tent, no fireplace, or anything. I look around and see that I'm in the middle of town. Men are cutting wood and tending to the fields while women are cooking and washing clothes in big buckets of brown-looking water.

"Where am I?" I ask, feeling lost, but no one replies; no one even looks up at me.

"Hello?" I call again, but everything goes on as if I'm not here.

I walk over to a house to peer in. Inside is a bed, a small wooden table with two chairs, and well, that's it.

"I guess they weren't into decorating much back in the day, huh," I say to myself. It's really actually a nice day. Some clouds, a slight breeze, a porridge-looking substance smelling rank cooks over a small fire in the center of the circle of dwellings, a door slams, and I hear a scream.

"No, Father, let her be!" screams a woman from one of the little dwellings.

"Dear daughter, you've known that little Virginia is...so special," a man cradling an infant says in smooth voice, a voice that seems oddly familiar.

"Father, you're mad! Put Virginia down, please!" the woman continues to beg, falling on her knees weeping.

"My darling daughter, you very well know what will happen otherwise," the man continues as their argument continues, handful of people from the other dwellings and gardens come to see the outburst.

"John, what is the meaning of this?" asks a tall muscular man with a rather long beard.

"You know exactly what must be done, Ananias!" shouts John. Murmurs go around the small crowd.

"Put Virginia down this instant, John. No one believes your nonsense!" shouts the man, his face turning red in anger.

"Now, now, no need to get upset. You know if she doesn't use her gift, bad things will come," says the man smoothly.

"Governor White, what is this all about?" asks another man who had just come from cutting wood.

"Governor?" I think aloud, but no one listens to me; they continue with their conversation.

"This is about how Virginia Dare is a witch," says John, still cradling baby Virginia in his arms.

"Impossible! She's only a child!" shouts the man.

"But I have proof!" shouts John. I imagine myself trudging over to them, but my legs don't carry out the task, so I'm left standing, watching them from afar.

"I have studied the sun for months now, and I have predicted that it will go out. Only she can save us!" he says.

"She cannot save anyone. She is a mere infant!" shouts Ananias angrily.

"Oh, but she can! And because I'm the only one who can help her channel her powers, I shall be called the king of the new world!" he exclaims, holding Virginia up higher so everyone can see her; she was the typical adorable baby—rosy cheeks and brilliant blue eyes.

"John, give me Virginia," says Ananias, holding out his arms.

"You have no place!" shouts John.

"I am her father!" Ananias shouts.

"Please, Father, Virginia cannot do what you want. She is not strong enough," says the woman who's supposedly Virginia's mother

"How dare you lie to me!" he shouts menacingly. Ananias moves to stand by his wife.

"Father, I am not lying. She can only prevent it for a little before her life wanes away along with her magic," she says loudly.

"Beloved wife, you know about this?" he asks, bewildered.

"Yes, unfortunately, she has been gifted for a destiny far greater than any of ours, but that destiny is to help mankind, not enslave it," says the wife. Ananias looks bewildered but still stands beside his wife protectively.

"Give us our daughter and leave!" shouts Ananias with authority.

"Not till I get what I desire," replies John darkly, holding up baby Virginia to the sun.

"Father, no! She is your granddaughter. Look at her, Her face already looks ashen," she says, still weeping.

"I am sorry, dear daughter, but this is my destiny," John says.

"Please, she is not strong enough, you will kill her, and you will not give mankind enough time to help our dying sun," she cries.

"Silence!" he shouts over the voices. "The time has come, and once I control the sun, I shall be forever known as a god!" he shouts, crazed.

"No! I will not allow it!" says Ananias, running up and elbowing John in the ribs and catching Virginia as he released her

"How dare you!" John roars angrily. "You shall pay for your arrogance!" He roars again, but now his eyes burn with fire, and sparks jump from his fingertips. He raises his arms, palms up.

"Watch out!" I scream at them terrified, but again, they can't hear me as fire shoots from his hands, burning the house behind them into ash.

"Father, stop!" screams the mother, but instead, he laughs hysterically, then burns another house. At first, the townspeople seem appalled. One of the many men gathered around charge with swords raised, but he merely flicks his wrist and they incinerate before his eyes.

"Stop, these are innocent people!" shouts Ananias, his face turning red with fury.

"Yes, but now all shall pay for denying me the gift!" replies John darkly, continuing to demolish the houses and any person who gets in the way.

"Please!" continues the mother, but he ignores her completely. Anger floods through me as I sprint toward him; I feel like smashing into him, breaking his hands so he can't hurt anyone anymore, but instead I stop in front of John.

"Stop or else!" I scream, but he only raises his hand and fires. I wait for pain, but when I look behind me, apparently the blast went right through me. John continues on bringing the house's down, literally.

"Cro-Croatoan," says a meek voice, and at first, I thought it was something different all together; but when I look over, baby Virginia is floating a foot above her mother's head all of a sudden, the words CRO are burned into a tree beside me. "Cro-Croatoan," Virginia says again in a wail, and the word *Croatoan* appears on a post near John. John lets out another roar.

"No, this cannot happen!" he proclaims, aiming his hands at little Virginia.

"No!" screams Ananias, running at John. That was that last thing he says before he's turned to ash.

"Ananias!" wails Virginia's mother.

"You...and the rest of this settlement will be over soon enough," he says in a shriek.

"Wait, please!" she says shakily, and then, everything goes dark. The towns people that were left all gasp as everything is plunged in darkness.

"See, see what you have created!" screams the mother in a shrill voice, tears streak her face; John falters and then falls to his knees. I look up at the baby. The poor thing looks seriously ill but is still floating, and then, it starts to seize. Just like Bay, the frail body was pulsating. *What is happening?!* I think, petrified.

The baby continues, then it drops a couple of feet; it regains itself, but soon falls completely. And within that second of little Virginia falling, the sun becomes bright and full, just like before...***She** bought us time*, I think to myself Eric lied. Before Virginia can crash, her mother catchers her in the crook of her arm, only fumbling slightly. With the mother's head down, and her other hand shielding Virginia's eyes, they run off deep into the woods.

Wait...this is Roanoke! So who then is Eric's many greats grandfather? Maybe it's Ananias. He definitely paid the price, but his only child was Virginia. A shudder runs through my spine. *Could it be John White? Does this mean Eric's evil too? Well, it wouldn't matter now though,* I say to myself, *he's dead.* My mind was escaping me like it knew all the answers before I could figure them out myself.

Wait, so the mother knew about her daughter being... special? And why would she hide it? Isn't that a good thing? I'm puzzled by this when I remember how bewildered Ananias looked when he found out. *Was that why? Or did she not want her father to know? And how come her own father betrayed her? Was it only for power?* Then a thought hits me, *Why did we never know?*

"Because there are no survivors," says a man behind me. I freeze. *Can he see me now?*

"Yes, I can," says the voice in reply. I turn to see John White standing behind me. "I always had truthfully."

"Why, why kill everyone?" I ask appalled.

"Well, if I can't rule them, I don't want little—hmm, what do you call it? Oh yes, tattle tales," he says with a smile.

"So what, you kill everyone, burn all the buildings, and leave? Blame it on some natives and pretend as if it never happened?" I ask with resentment.

"Well, not necessarily, if you must know, after I kill everyone, I continue my secret research on the whereabouts of when the sun will again die. Unfortunately, the Indians saw me. I couldn't take my chances. I left for England knowing I would need to be back again. I made up some silly excuse, and of course as expected, my research fails. The cursed

Spanish Armada stops me for a time, but I return. Eventually, I come back to Roanoke. Never did figure it out. So I continue with my art, start a new colony, and eventually die when I'm old and ripe," he says without much feeling.

"Wait, if you killed everyone, how did you get the crew?" I ask, puzzled.

"Dear boy, I burn a whole village with my hands, and you ask me how I summon a crew? Pity. I thought you were the one," he says gloomily. I feel my cheeks burn.

"Well, you didn't kill everyone," I say, remembering Virginia and her mother.

"Oh, yes…my daughter and Virginia. Well, if they don't die in the forest, they'll keep their mouths shut… unless they want to be burned at the stake for being a witch," he says nonchalantly. My breath catches in my throat.

"You still do those?" I asked, scared of the thought.

"Still do them! Witch hunting has been around since ancient Egypt. They didn't stop till the late seventeenth century although the burnings were a little later. I left Roanoke around 1587. But the cost still hangs heavy. Bad things happen to witches," he continues coolly.

"But is she really a witch?" I ask, knowing that almost no one was actually a witch in the trials, all made-up charges and what not from their husbands...

"No, of course not. It's a gift, a 'superpower,' if you will. She was the first baby born in the one place where the fabric would thin and knot. She was chosen, powers given to her by the force of the universe, an unseen balance that protects time," he says.

"So this unseen balance, did it choose us too?" I ask, finally getting answers.

"I suspect most of you were. But Bay must be an ancestor. Her powers are so much like Virginia's, it can't be coincidental," he replies.

"Okay, so were we chosen when we were Virginia's age, or just now? How come we only started noticing our powers the day before we were kidnapped?" I ask.

"Who knows when you were chosen. All of you were probably chosen at different times, and when your powers are needed they will appear, like now for instance," he explains. It all makes sense now.

"So how do we do it? Save the fabric, I mean," I ask, hoping I will get a straight answer for once.

"Your theory on the black hole is spot on. In fact, I wish I would've thought of that," he says with a smile

"Okay, so how do we make it then?" I specify.

"Think about it. What did Virginia say to prevent it?" he asks.

"I don't think I have the power to fly," I say, confused.

"No! What did she say? It's much like what Bay must do," he says, irritated.

"You mean the Cro-Croatoan thing?" I ask. "And why does Bay talk in Greek?"

"Yes, now think. If she says that and there isn't a black hole, then What should you say so there is one?" he continues.

"The opposite of that? Why is that so powerful? And what about Bay?" I ask, now officially confused

"Exactly, but don't ask too many questions. The words are less important. It's the people who say it, taking that... leap of faith. And as for Bay, she just hasn't learned how to control her power. I highly suspect if she didn't say things—in any language—her mind would overload, and/or possibly unwind itself. But she will understand. She is a descendant of me after all," he says, giving me a wink

"Well, then how do you know all these things about your future if you haven't lived it?" I ask still pondering.

"This is your dream, so to me, it sounds like you managed to figure it out all on your own," he says with a smile and a wink, then he and the whole scenery starts to dissolve.

"No, wait!" I yell.

"Remember," he says, "it's eleven thirty!" He says this in a voice that sounds like—

"Josh, wake up! Its eleven thirty! We only have half an hour till this whole place goes boom!" shouts Valery, shaking me awake.

"Huh?" I look up at her through squinted eyes, the light felt too bright.

"Get up!" she yells one last time.

"Okay, okay, I'm up," I say sleepily. "I had the weirdest dream...What was it again?" I say to myself, completely blanking.

"Come on!" she shouts again, pulling me up.

"I got it, I'm coming," I say, holding my hands out defensively.

"Well, hurry, everyone's around the tree that has the CRO written on it," she says.

"Well, that makes sense," I say to myself as we run to where the others are at.

BAY TINE

We're nearing the time of doomsday, and every second that ticks by feels like another kick to the stomach; Andrew, sensing my nervousness, reassuringly grasps my hand.

"Thanks," I whisper.

"No problem," he replies in a whisper too.

"Are you nervous?" I ask. *What a stupid question!*

"No," he says, surprising me. "We know exactly what to do, what is there to worry about?"

"Hmm…very convincing," I say, still not that convinced, but I gave him a smile; and he didn't press any further.

"Okay, guys, while Bay creates the black hole, Josh, make sure you're shielding everyone. Then, Valery, when you sense everyone's getting a little stretchy, you work on that. Adam, you're going to transport things we might need on short notice. Timmy, you are going to be constantly reading Bay's mind to make sure she's okay. Chelsey, with your speed, you're going to run around Bay. This will help with the black hole. Henry, you keep your eye on the future, and, Jessica, try to get anything in the air safely on the ground. Olivia, you need to watch for guards with me so nothing gets interrupted. And, Andrew, why don't you help keep Bay safe?" says Stan seriously.

"Hey, what about me?" asks Lilia, moaning.

"You're going to help Olivia and me," he replies confidently.

"Fine, sure, whatever," gripes Lilia.

"You guys ready? We have about twenty minutes," says Stan, ignoring Lilia.

"Yeah," I say meekly.

"Okay, well, get into position. And if anything happens, meet at this tree," he says, pointing to the tree with the word *CRO* on it. Everyone nods, and we get to it.

I had a strange dream last night; I can't really remember it either, but I could still remember the feeling of pure terror and Eric's words, "*As for my many greats grandfather, let's just say he gave us some time before the beginning of the end, but Roanoke had to pay the price.*" I shiver at the thought.

Then an idea itches at the back of my mind. *What if this whole place blows? Like nothing was left of Roanoke...* I try to shake the thought, but it sticks to me. *I'm the only one strong enough to make the black hole. They can go somewhere else to make sure the airplanes and what not are on the ground. They can't sacrifice their lives for something I have to do alone.*

I want to deny it, I want them here, all of them, willing to be the big superheroes, but I can't do that to them. I won't do that to them. I won't have anything if this thing works, but they have lots ahead of them. *I have to do this...alone.*

"You guys! I, I had a vision!" I scream. Josh, Andrew, Valery, Timmy, and Chelsey are the first ones to arrive, then there's Adam, and eventually as time ticks by Stan, Lilia, Olivia, and Jessica all file in.

"You guys, we're at the wrong doomsday!" I say exasperatingly. I know I have to really believe this to work since we have a human lie detector here.

"Are you sure?" asks Lilia, a bit surprised.

"Yeah, I know, I saw something. It's all the way in Colorado. We have to leave now!" I exclaim, everyone's a bit hesitant, but they don't argue.

"Okay, where exactly is it? I will transport us there. We don't have any time to waste now," replies Adam so kindly I almost lose my nerve.

"At the...astronomical clock," I say rushed.

"Okay, guys, hold on," he says, but I secretly take a step back. And in an instant, they are gone, leaving me all alone.

Don't come back for me...This is my job. Good-bye. I concentrate to Timmy and make sure I don't get sucked into Adam's transportation vortex; well, it sounded better in my own head.

"Okay, I can do this. No fear, only power," I say to myself while thinking of Andrew, how he wasn't even the least bit scared. "I can do this!" I yell then I focus on a little black sphere, something so compressed it basically eats everything in its path. I think the black hole before me, building, building, building until it's huge. I resist the spasms. I resist the pain. I can do this. I can channel the energy through thoughts, not pain.

I open my eyes to see a tiny black mass growing bigger more round. I smile, relieved. I'm doing it! I want to shout, but I can't break my concentration.

"Very nicely done, Bay. I knew you would sacrifice yourself for your friends," says a voice behind me. I let out a shriek and turn to see the one and only.

It was Eric Nova.

"I thought you were dead!" I exclaim. I wasn't sure if I should be relieved or worried.

"Yes, you *thought* I was, didn't you?" he says with a merry laugh.

"That's not funny! You left us all alone to save the world, and you could've helped!" I shout at him.

"Oh, but if I would've told you about your powers, do you think you would've been as experienced?" he asks smoothly.

"Yes! We could've practiced! We could've known how to control them!" I shout upset. "We could've saved the world before it came to this!" I shout, but my voice cracks, and I almost fall into tears.

"Oh, my dear, you still haven't figured it out?" he asks, looking shocked.

"Figure what out!" I spit back at him.

"I never wanted you to…create this black hole to save the planet. I wanted you to work on your powers enough so you would be strong enough to fix the circle itself," he says with a sly smile. "And once you do that, I will be able to make or break it whenever, and however, I please!" he continues. "Then the entire world will bow at my feet, for I will be their savior, their ruler! I will be in complete and utter control! Just think, no more war, no more political battles, everything…perfect," he says manically.

"Circles have to end, you said so yourself! And if you're going to be *their savior*, how come you can't fix it yourself?" I ask, sure it was a stupid question, but I had to stall.

"Ah, silly child, circles don't end. They are forever, I simply gave you a very…easy way to think about it. But unlike you, my power is immunity, your petty powers are useless on me. Unfortunately, I do not have your power to control things, like the circles," he says happily.

"Okay, so what's in it for me?" I ask, still stalling.

"Hmm…I don't know. If you do this for me, I suppose I can let you live," he says in my ear, holding a gun to my temple.

"You're a sick man," I spit furiously.

"So be it, but I will rule, I will bring glory back to my grandfather and have the wealthiest and longest dynasty in the history of the world!" he says evilly.

"I…dare…you," I say, showing no fear. He can't kill me; he needs me.

"If you wish, you see, I either rule or this whole universe will go down. Take your pick," he says unperturbedly.

"I'd rather have all of space turn into nothing than be ruled by someone who is greedy and will only enslave us. It won't be a life worth living in the first place," I say then I do something so brave and so undeniably stupid, that it couldn't have been me doing it. But I am, and I do. I turn around and face him, stare him in the eye, and pull his trigger.

"No! How dare you!" he exclaims as I fall to the ground.

Guys, it's your turn now...good-bye was my last thought...then everything was bright white; and in another instant, everything's dark, yet I felt strangely alive. Unable to think or move or talk, I felt nothing but darkness, yet I still felt...not dead.

ANDREW NEDSON

It's so weird leaving only fifteen minutes before doomsday. I wonder what Bay saw exactly and why Henry didn't see it first, which brought up that bad feeling, like the thought of him being a traitor, but why would someone sabotage saving the world? I want to know, but I don't at the same time. Shivering at the thought, I reach for Bay's hand, but she wrenches her hand out of mine, and before I can even look at her for an explication, she slaps me with so much force I started seeing stars in one eye and the whole right side of my face stung.

"What was that!" yells Lilia. I'm dumbstruck.

"Hurts, huh," remarks Adam bitterly, and Lilia smiles innocently at him.

"Sorry, thought you were Bay. She was right beside me," I say, looking around; panic grips me as I search the heads…eleven.

"You guys, she's not here," says Timmy

"I kind of got that. Adam, take us back, now!" I say, feeling our whole plan crumble before it even starts.

"No!" shouts Timmy. "Well, what I mean is…Well, she sent me a thought," he clarifies.

"Well, feel free to share it," I say my panic level steadily increasing with every second.

"She thought: *Don't come back for me... This is my job. Good-bye*," he says sadly.

"What!" I exclaim. "She's going to try it all alone!" I feel like I'm drowning. I can't catch my breath, and I am trying as hard as I can not to bawl. Timmy puts a hand on my arm in perfect understanding.

"Wait, so are we going back or not?" asks Adam. I look him straight in the eye and smile.

"We're going back," I say.

"Wait...What time is it?" asks Jessica.

"I don't know. Is it really that important?" I ask in return, only thinking about Bay.

"Well, duh! If she's doing her thing, and we land right on top of her, it could mean—*boom*!" she says quickly.

"Just tell her the time numbskulls," retorts Lilia.

"Um...ten to twelve," says Stan.

"We only have a few minutes," replies Valery bluntly.

"No, we have ten," I say, confused.

"No, it takes eight minutes for the sun to reach earth, so we need that black hole to be in outer space before that sun blows up or else we're all toast, remember???" Valery says hastily.

"Adam, get us to Roanoke!" shouts Olivia over everyone. And by instinct I hold on to whoever's around me—which isn't always a good idea—but that's my power, freaking awesome reflexes. Then, poof. We're magically in Roanoke. I don't know how he does it, but it is so cool.

"Bay?" says Timmy as we hear a gunshot.

"Oh my god, Bay!" I say, but it was filled with grief, that gunshot, it was meant for Bay…and it hit its target.

"Bay!" I say, rushing to her aid but I'm stopped. "Eric?" I ask, confusion and anger pushing for dominance.

"Why hello, Andrew, been a while, hasn't it?" replies Eric smoothly.

"You…you killed her. You killed Bay!" I yell furiously.

"Actually, she killed herself. What a pity actually," he replies, looking down at Bay's crumpled form.

"Liar! You killed her, and now, I'm going to kill you!" I scream, angrily charging at him, only thinking of one thing: kill. Only seeing one thing: red.

But before I can stop him, Chelsey appears in front of me. I stop on a dime and am about to run around her when Chelsey moves too.

"Look, Andrew, I know you care about her, but it's over. We have to focus on the rest of the world now," she says hastily. *But Bay is my world!* I want to protest, then I think about the pictures she showed me during one of her little episodes. I feel like I know her more than she knows herself, and I think she feels the same about me.

"Come on, Andrew, the faster we save the world, the better chance of her surviving," yells Valery from the group. I didn't quite understand what she meant, but if it meant a chance, then I'm in.

"What about Eric?" I ask, looking at him coldly. He still had that gun. Chelsey nods, and in a blur, she's over and back to me with his gun; Eric looks stunned, but I had gotten sort of accustomed to it now that she had done it several times.

"Better," I say, running back to the group.

"I'm sorry," whispers Timmy. I blush and try to forget what I had thought, embarrassed at what he might know. *Jeez, a little privacy*, I think for a second, like seriously, having to live with a mind reader for a couple days is like having to use the bathroom, but it has no doors. But I can't stay mad for long because soon enough my mind drifts back to Bay.

"Andrew!" yells Josh.

"Huh?" I say, snapping back into focus.

"I think if we all hold hands and say, Croation-Cro, then we can do what we originally planned to do... but without Bay," he says, now just him mentioning her name is like lemon juice to a cut.

"Why?" I ask dumbfounded.

Josh huffs. "There's not enough time for talking. I'll tell you later," he says, and with that, we begin, in a circle around the tree with the word *CRO* engraved in it we start chanting, and before too long, a large black blob appears from the tree, it gets bigger and bigger and bigger until it shoots upward so fast it looks like a streak of black.

I feel exhausted, and when Olivia and Timmy let go of my hands, I nearly fall to the ground.

"We...did...it," I say happily then I black out.

CHELSEY O'NEIL

It took all of my energy, which is surprising, since all we had to do was hold hands and say Croation-Cro. But still it felt as if every ounce of energy was coursing through me, building in my chest then through my hands, and then it was gone; I vaguely remember what happened, since I almost passed out too. But once the black hole of despair launched into space, everything seems a little brighter. Well, actually that was the sun blowing up. If we would've done it a second later, we might not be here now is all I can think of.

In awe, I watch as the black hole travels up till it's hardly visible. Still growing, it starts to dip in the opposite direction of the explosion. Huh? The sun turns black. Thank goodness for the moon and some of the stars bathing the place in its pale silvery light or else it would've been pitch-black.

Just barely able to see it, the sun/black hole dashes across the horizon to meet the other black hole. Then our black hole does the same.

"Um…guys, I don't know about you, but if we're not in the middle before those two crash, we're all going to turn to noodles," I say alarmed.

"Adam, can you transport...all of earth? Only a hundred feet away from the two of them, then we should be able to do exactly what we talked about," says Josh calmly.

"Um...I guess I could try?" says Adam in a shaky tone.

"Okay...you've got this," replies Josh encouragingly. And then...*poof*. All of a sudden, the two distant black holes are a whole lot bigger, like twice the size of earth bigger. Wind whips my hair in every direction, and the force of their vacuuming suction almost defies gravity, pulling me off the ground.

"Josh!" Valery yells, Josh nods and closes his eyes, then in a minute, everything just stops. I land hard on the ground with a yelp as my legs buckle under me.

"Chelsey, you okay?" asks Valery, putting a hand on my leg, automatically healing it.

"Yep!" I say a bit grumpily. I guess I had thought it would be a lot...longer...harder... more complicated? I couldn't find the appropriate word to describe what I was feeling, but before I could focus for long, I was pulled into another problem.

"Chelsey, I need your help," says Valery, struggling to lift Bay's limp body.

"Um...I get a bit queasy around blood," I say nervously, that, and I didn't want to be anywhere near her when Andrew woke up.

"Chelsey!" she says again, agitated.

"Fine, I'm coming," I say, running in a blur.

"Okay, I need your help lifting her," she says, instructing me to grab her feet, "We'll move her to the tree. Over there my powers feel really strong," she explains lamely.

"Yeah, okay," I say, pulling her feet. We get to the tree and set her down. Valery is already working on her head, but it's not working.

"Maybe..." I hesitate. "Maybe she's too far gone?" I say as respectfully as I can.

"No, she's not," says Timmy confidently. "She's not thinking, but there's something...alive about her in there. It's not some hollow shell, trust me," he says again.

"Okay, okay, I trust you," I say, only a little skeptical.

"I do too...She feels alive, she's just not..." Valery falters.

"Breathing?" I say, finishing her sentence.

"Yeah," Valery says with a frown. She continues working, and I feel like our hopes for Bay is quickly fading away, but Valery doesn't give up, and I focus all my energy to her, but nothing works. She was dead.

"Why look at what the little band of misfits have accomplished," sneers Eric.

"You! You killed her!" shouts Valery. "You sicken me." She basically spits in his face; I grab her arm, restraining her.

"But my dear, you have your facts wrong...like I said before, she pulled the trigger of my gun, not me," he says with a snide, evil smile.

"She wouldn't do that," says Timmy in a whisper, obviously disbelieving.

"Oh, but she would, and she did," he says happily.

"Why are you even here? It's all over. Any second our world will be completely safe," I say, feeling my blood boil. "And until that last second, it will go on without a hitch!" I say, feeling my power running through my veins, making my fingers tingle and my eyes fierce.

"You don't scare me," he says happily.

"Do I now?" I say, running in a blur behind him; it really tired me out to go so fast, but now, I couldn't stop. He looks slightly frightened by my appearing act, but he quickly hides it.

"Funny, I thought you had speed, not transportation," he says coolly. I run in front of him, my face only inches from his.

"No, its speed" I say, then run behind him. "More powerful than your little test results showed you, huh?" I say then I run so fast I'm basically running up a tree.

"Stop that, fight me like a…" He falters.

"Like a man?" I say with a laugh. This only makes him look angry. "Oh, with pleasure," I say, fury punctuating every word.

"No," says a meek voice. "Let me," she says. I look down from the tree.

"Bay!" I yell, feeling an imaginary weight lift off my shoulders.

"Ah yes, the girl with all heart and no brains," sneers Eric.

"Shut up or you're getting your butt kicked twice as hard," she says, holding up double fists; he smirks, but I had a funny feeling he didn't want to say anything that would provoke her.

"You are scared of us," says Bay plaintively. "You thought you could shape us, thought you could get us to do your bidding just by putting a gun to our heads," she says, her voice getting louder. "But you're wrong," she says, and without seizure, without screaming ancient Greek whatever, she creates a ball of light; it was so bright you couldn't even see darkness. There wasn't even a shadow—only light.

Then as it grew bigger and bigger in her hands, she looks up at him and smiles.

"Any last words?" she asks playfully.

"I'll be back, this isn't over! Not yet anyway," he says.

"Strange last words," she sneers, then with the flick of her wrist, *poof*, he's gone.

"It's over," I say from the tree, but Bay only looks away in disgust.

"If I can come back…so can he" is all she says before walking over in the darkness to the relative area of where Andrew is. And I'll leave that part for someone else to explain.

I avoid that area and head directly to where I hear Josh and Adam debating about what they should tell the press.

"Well, they're going to want to know something!" I hear Adam complain.

"Yeah, and the minute we say something, one, they either think we've gone insane and we end up in a psychiatric ward, or we end up science experiments," argues Josh.

"Or superheroes!" replies Adam.

"True…I just don't want the other possibilities," he says.

There's a long silence and then I pipe in, "What about an anonymous tip to a local news station?"

"You know...that's a good idea," says Adam.

"Yeah, I guess...but no names," says Josh.

"Yeah, yeah, okay, grandpa," I say, happy to finally be of some use to someone.

"Ha, ha, it's so funny I forgot to laugh," he says grumpily.

"I know right!" I say sarcastically hyper. "Hey...how did you know what to say, like Croation-Cro? That isn't exactly something you say every day," I clarify.

"Well, I had this dream, but when I woke up, I couldn't remember it at all...at least, not till I saw Eric, then it all flooded back to me," he begins hesitantly, then he goes into how he was in old timey Roanoke and about little baby Virginia and what she said to have prevented the black hole and his theory about reversing it. *Hmm, maybe I should pay more attention in history class.*

"So you based this all on a guess from a dream?" asks Stan incredulously.

"Well, an educated guess," corrects Josh weakly, and as he continued talking, everyone started gathering around; I didn't even know that everyone was around until Stan lit a fire.

After he finishes, I look at the sky, absorbing the odd but very interesting story...then I realize, it's still pitch-black.

"You guys!" I shout. Everyone looks at me expectantly. "The sky!" I say, pointing, and they don't even have to ask; a chill runs through the groups, and I didn't have to be a mind reader to know what they were thinking, and I was thinking of it too. *Did we do it wrong?*

"You guys, it's okay," assures Bay. "Think about it, some things changed forever, the sun being one of them...especially since it became a black hole and devoured the rest of the fabric of time and space while we got away at the last second," she says in a bit of exaggeration.

"Well, I don't know about you, but I'd rather not go into another ice age," comments Lilia, grumpy like always.

"I know, I know," says Bay, standing up and closing her eyes, and again, she makes that ball of fire, that intense glowing sphere of pure colorful light. I felt as though just being next to it would burn off all my hair. Just like that, with incredible speed, it shot up into the sky and bursts into millions of shining stars. But those soon fade out when the biggest star of all (hint to the dummies; the sun) forms above us, and the brilliant blue sky appears. And once again, the birds in their trees begin to chirp. I half expected some big celestial choir to be singing the day was so perfect.

"Okay, I'm not even going to ask," comments Andrew after Bay sits back down; he holds her hand and scoots closer to her

"So...this is...it?" asks Henry.

"Yeah, I think it is," says Jessica.

"I never thought I would say this...but I'll miss you guys," comments Lilia.

"Aw, shucks, good thing I'm coming back with you!" says Adam sarcastically, then he does something even an insane person wouldn't do. Probably the bravest thing I've ever seen. He leans in and kisses her, probably he longest, sweetest kiss I've ever witnessed between two twelve year olds; it's still the strangest thing I've seen all day. That, and she doesn't beat the crap out of him. She doesn't even shrug him off.

"What is this world coming to!" says Timmy dramatically.

"Shut up, stupid," says Olivia, smacking the back of his head.

"Yep, I'm totally going to miss this," says Stan sarcastically.

"Come on, you know you love us," says Valery happily.

"Yeah, and I love chicken too, but do you see me getting all emotional with them? Yeah that's what I thought," says Stan gruffly, and with that, we all crack up. A laugh that has been missing for a long time.

"You guys, I know you think this is it…but I have one of those feelings that this is only the beginning," says Bay sullenly after the laughing had died down.

"Yeah, but we'll be ready when that comes," says Jessica.

"Yeah, we saved the whole freaking world," Lilia points out.

"And Bay beat the crap out of Eric," adds Timmy, "and he said that he was immune to us." Everyone goes quiet.

"Is that why you think it's not over?" asks Valery. "You think he's just…pretending to be dead?" asks Valery.

"Well, sort of. But even if my powers were stronger and he did die, we still have to be ready for the next beginning of the end," replies Bay.

"And we will," says Adam.

"Yeah!" says everyone. Bay smiles, she still seems troubled, but I don't want to press her.

"Wait, don't you find it funny that he didn't try to stop us...like when we were making that black hole?" asks Jessica quietly.

"I figure he chickened out. He wants to live as much as the next guy, and when he realized we would give our lives for it, he backed off," says Bay confidently.

"Yeah, that makes sense," says Andrew, smiling at Bay.

"But why did he show up at the end, like wouldn't he just run off?" asks Jessica again.

"Ego," I pipe in; everyone nods in agreement.

"Well, we should head out, don't want to worry the folks," says Bay sadly. Andrew wraps one arm around her waist. And before I could ask what that was about, I realize. Bay doesn't have anyone.

"Bay—"

"It's okay, I'm fine," says Bay, interrupting me. I let go of the topic not wanting to hurt her feelings or anything, so instead, I look at everyone's scruffy dirty hair with their torn clothes all laughing like the world was never in danger at all. And I feel myself apart of them. *No more life-size Barbie*, I think with a smile as we all say our good-byes.

"Okay, I'm going to drop off Timmy and Olivia first, then Henry and Jessica. Then I'll drop off Bay and Andrew, and then Josh, Valery, and Chelsey. After that, I'll drop off Stan. Sound good?" asks Adam.

"Yeah, but I'm going to take the limo back," says Stan, winking at Olivia.

After everyone nods in agreement, he shouts, "Okay then, hold on!" And *poof*, we're off, and after a while, I'm in my bed sleeping till who knows how long. My mom and sister are basically fawning over me asking me what happened and how I got away.

I said that Chase was forced to take me hostage, but I ran away, and that I had no clue where he was. And neither did anyone in the entire world apparently, according to my mom. *I wonder why?*

So life for me is great. I ended up selling my Ferrari for some cash to buy some killer running shoes, and I started track, beating every record that Trina had set. Life is good in Chelseyland, at least as far as I know. But I still check my bedroom window before I go to bed, and I always check people's eyes before getting in a car with them.

My End.

OLIVIA THOMPSON

School never sounded so appealing, and a bed felt like I was in heaven, and well, food was something else. The minute I got home, I almost regretted it. Don't get me wrong, seeing my parents again was almost as good as food. But I really hated lying, though I didn't want to go to a nuthouse either. Plus, if they believed me—not likely—I would never leave my room again.

So the story went like this:

Timmy and I were running late so we had to go on the bike trail that wasn't exactly safe…then I said I crashed. After Timmy had reached me, a man came out of the forest and stuffed something in our faces. I was out cold. Then the rest was a blur. And after what seems like eternity, he just took us back to the woods, and we hiked back.

It wasn't completely true, but it was enough to keep my parents from worrying too much. So after they had us checked out for any type of infection, drug, and whatnot, finally we were home with enough flowers and balloons to float the whole house. Timmy got pretty popular too, and since we went through a traumatic event, they are letting us take the rest of the week off school, and we don't have to make up the work. Sometimes it feels like I need to be kidnapped more often.

My parents, on the other hand, made a huge effort to clean up the trail and put rails to make it safer. They also give donations to every agency that covers recovering kidnapped children across the United States. That and until one of us gets our driver's license, we're never riding our bikes to school again.

My Fantabulous Ending

TIMMY THOMPSON

So yeah, Olivia summed everything up pretty nicely…

Although, she did leave out the part about how Stan gave an anonymous tip about how two unexpected black holes had broken down our universe and that we're the first humans to ever do anything of this nature. The news definitely used it, and science proves it, the stars and galaxies look like they went through a blender. Some are like a hundred light-years closer and vice versa. *I guess Bay was never into astronomy*

But that only makes science more interesting in my opinion, as long as nothing terrible happens. But it seems like everything in our new galaxy is safe. So why worry? That's really all I can think to say when I hear people thinking/talking about that.

The cool thing is, is that we still have our powers, so that's a bonus. And it's really nice when I get stuck on a test question to be able to read some of the smarter people's minds and put down the right answer. Yeah, I know it's cheating, but my grades are at an all-time high, and this is helpful if I want to take early classes at some community colleges when I'm older.

The downside though is that you know what other people think about you, and sometimes this is good, like I know that Andrew Nedson thinks I'm a *freaking genius*. And of course, I can mock Olivia for thinking that I'm a really good brother since she actually says this in her mind—who would've known! But knowing that Lilia thinks that I have a rat face and I should stay out of people's brains is a bit harsh, but I don't take it personally, she's a naturally grouchy person. But also friends at school seem a little less appealing; my best friend actually thinks that I should be held back since I'm cruddy at everything. That and he thinks I'm super wimpy. Well, he was very surprised when I quoted him on that…but that's another story…

My Somewhat Random Ending

ANDREW NEDSON

Going home was like a slice of heaven. I know from now on that I have to show how much everyone means to me since you never know when you'll be secretly selected to save the world and then you'll be shipped off into space before you even get to say bye.

My family is so cool. When I get home, I'm wrapped into a family hug and my mom makes a thanksgiving feast in honor of my return. And the best part in my mind, they didn't ask about anything; they said that all they care about is that I'm home safe and that Bay is okay too.

So I go back to school not expecting anything big, but when I get there, my whole homeroom has a big "*Welcome back Andrew*" sign, and everyone pops out and gives me a hug.

I go through the rest of the day hugging people and struggling to catch up on class work. I think the only time I felt truly relaxed was the last class of the day, being able to play and feel the music vibrating off the walls and the ground, and all the way up my legs and rattling in my brain. Now that might not sound awesome, but you really have to try it to understand.

About twenty minutes before school ended there was a knock at the door, and there in the flesh is Bay Tine. I almost fall off my chair, at first I thought it wasn't her, since she was supposed to go to Oregon and what not, but taking a double look, she was definitely there; she looked so calm and casual. I wanted to hug her and tell her that I had missed her, saying good-bye as Adam dropped her off was hard enough, but now. I didn't know what to think

As Bay walks to her seat, she brushes up against me, and just at her touch, the images she gave me when she was first figuring out her powers blink in my head, only long enough to get the feeling, but not long enough to really hold on to them. When I look down, in my hand there's a note:

I'm staying

That's all it said, but reading it made my heart race and my lips curve into a smile. I look back at her, and she gives me thumbs-up; and for the rest of the day, my head is in the clouds.

We all changed during this whole ordeal. I guess knowing how short life is really puts things in perspective, everyone else seems so immature now, and I know things will be a lot different. But at the same time, it feels like everything will be more normal than ever. And whatever happens, I'm ready to take it all in stride. Does that sound really cheesy? Okay, well, umm…rock on!

My Super Happy Ending

ADAM SHARD

So all goes back to normal, well actually, it's really the opposite. Lilia is a whole lot nicer, and we hang out all the time, whether it's going to Hawaii, Greenland, or just the movies. Yeah, my powers are pretty cool like that.

After getting everyone back, I finally went home and sleep till my family finds me under my covers snoring lightly. My dad even joked that I was probably sleeping there the whole time. Now I probably did the stupidest thing ever and told them the whole thing; everything about Eric, the black hole, and my powers. But before I could even show them the proof, they took me to a psychiatrist and left me for an hour.

Of course when I took the shrink out to sushi… in Japan, she finally believed me; and since my family insisted on these appointments, we struck a deal that we would get lunch every other week, and she would give complimentary appointments and assure my parents that everything was fine and that went on for a while. She was actually pretty fluent in like five languages; it's amazing what you learn about people when you take them to every country in Europe.

So I never did lie, but no one really believed me in the first place. So I never really mentioned it again, and I really actually didn't mind because in all truth, one, I didn't want to worry my family. And two, I didn't want someone spilling the beans to a government agent or whatever and get shipped off to area 51.

So all was hectic, but I have actually found that I like it that way. So all is good in my kind of crazy way.

My Hectic but Freaking Awesome Ending

STAN PRICE

So after I personally give back the couple's limo—which by the way is really hard since I didn't know where they were in the first place. Adam drops me off at the station. I half expected to be carried into a dank cell wearing handcuffs and an orange jumpsuit. But instead I find myself being held in a hug by E. J. Apparently, they made a mistake. And while I was gone, they had caught the guys who broke into the prison, and the people who set us up—which happened to be the same people—so all our criminal records were expunged and sealed tight. In the end, I still had a job, and E. J. was back to his regular goofy self.

I was allowed a couple days off to make sure I could cool off. And after I ate enough to break the scale in my bathroom, I was back on the force. And from then on, I somehow always got the easiest crooks since their car would miraculously overheat when they would try to get away in their cars. Of course, that was only...luck. It was life as I like it once again in the big CA, and really, I couldn't ask for anything better at the moment.

My Short and Sweet Ending

JOSH WILLIAMS

Okay, if you can believe it, the minute I get home my sister basically runs over me. Like full on football tackle, I hate to admit it too, but it was a really good hit, now you might be like what the heck? *You've been gone for days and your sister beats the crap out of you?* Thankfully it wasn't like that, it was more of a really, really rough hug. After, she starts asking rapid-fire questions while somehow telling me everything that had happened since I had left at the same time. Then, she shows me her grade on the assignment she did all by herself. It was an A-, but it was really awesome from where she was before. After congratulating her, my parents basically do the same thing as my sister and tackle me in a hug.

After a couple days everything settled down a bit, and ironically, the first thing my sis points out is my perfect tan since I don't have my force field/sun screen on 24-7—at least I never need sunscreen. I could almost imagine an infomercial about it:

These Inviso shields are easy to apply, and you don't even feel it! That and it protects everything from insane robot bullies to UVA and UVB rays!

Okay, lame, sure. But I've never been a really cool person anyway. After this whole thing was over, Valery and I hang out pretty often. Constantly practicing our powers and finding different ways to use them so it's almost a completely different power altogether. When we said we would be prepared; Valery and I really took it to heart.

School has been better than ever; I only do my homework, and I sit with the robotics club kids. I don't even go to robotics anymore, but I've found that they can hold really interesting conversations, and occasionally, Valery will hang with us too. All feels done and over, and so for the time being, I rest easy.

My Ultimate Happy Ending!

VALERY JACKSON

So when I get home my mom freaks out, I guess she had taken the two weeks I had been gone off from work and basically lived in the police station, constantly checking for any news on my case. Of course, they didn't connect the twelve different missing people to being the reason for the world to still be spinning around the sun, figures.

But now that everything has gone its way, it's nice to know that I am not average, not the typical girl on the block or some random genius either. But someone with powers that defy all the laws of everything. Well, finding out that you have super powers and were made to save the fabric of time, makes you want to go out of your way to defy the odds in whatever way you can.

All in all, saving the world was a mountain worth climbing, and I don't have to be a mind reader or fortune-teller to know that the next mountain is going to be bigger. And when it's time to climb it, we'll be ready.

My Dramatic End

JESSICA RISE

Everything is still a bit crazy at school, and even my least favorite teacher threw me a big welcome back party in the class that day. After that, of course, Henry and I just hung out by ourselves eating cake and giving the occasional hug to a person who I hardly know in the first place. You know, I've always wondered what everyone would think about me if I died or about to be dead anyway. Like, would they cry for me? Be happy I'm gone? Would they feel sorry for me? Or be glad it wasn't them…or all of the above? But after this whole thing, I really don't care as long as I'm alive. Now I love being back, but I still uneasy feeling. Like, I could never stand not running in the halls. Or not going outside or even just having to wear safety goggles because there is a candle lit in the science classroom. But now, everything makes me nervous, every little sound makes me want to jump out the window. It's not over. If it were, I wouldn't be so antsy; I just wish it would be so I could get back to my life.

To cover up my newfound twitchy nature, I just say that a man approached Henry and I and eventually we were in triple D, and there was a huge hole, and as we could dodge the guy's blade, we fell in. We only survived by holding on to some roots and climbing out.

Sometimes I feel like someone's going to ask what happened, and I tell them a different story than what I've been telling everyone. I hate lying, and I would never do it unless it was to keep everyone safe, and since Bay was so freaked about Eric not being dead, I don't want to have to pull anyone into my fate.

My Selfless Ending

HENRY TUCKER

I was fine. After Adam dropped us off by triple D, we took a quick look at that hole we had once fell in. I don't know why I thought about letting go in the beginning. The most confusing thing is that I saw this exact moment; I had seen myself looking down at this hole right now thinking about how I was glad I let go, but then, that means I can see a lot farther than just a week. So are my powers stronger than I had originally thought, or was that all Eric?

For a long time, I sensed that people were skeptical about me, about my powers, how I didn't see that the sun was so far gone or that Eric would come to Roanoke or about not knowing that Bay was tricking everyone. But I really don't have an explanation for that. I guess the future I see was always meant to happen, but that doesn't mean I was keeping it from everyone; it was just that I never had a perfectly clear picture till it actually happened.

Seeing me here from nearly two weeks ago is so mind-boggling to me. Eventually, I just pass it off as a miracle and go on my merry way, but I think there will always be another part of me. Always itching for an explanation, but the great thing I learned about the future is that it hasn't happened yet, we still have all our lives to do whatever we want. And right now, I feel like spending a little time just enjoying the crazy spin of everything and smelling some roses on the way.

My Short yet Inspirational Ending

BAY TINE

I had Adam drop me off at my house. The house I grew up in. Leaving feels like something that I shouldn't even have to consider.

Cautiously, I walk up the steps, stretch to reach the key on top of the door, then taking a breath, I turn the lock. I don't know what I expected, maybe an empty house, maybe something worse (like maybe Eric in the house trying to scare me), but instead I come in and I'm hit with the all too familiar cinnamon and flower sent. Before I had always hated that combination, but now, it made the house feel all the more welcoming.

The lights were on and the house looked cleaner than ever. I ran my finger on the dining room table, only to come back with a clean hand.

"Hello?" I say a bit quietly. "Anyone here?" I ask louder. I hear scuffling footsteps from the stairs, then as they become louder and louder, I tense, bracing myself for the worst.

"Bay!" shrieks my mom. "Bay! Is that you?" she exclaims in disbelief.

"I—I thought you were…"

"Same here," I say before she can finish, and I run to her and hug her so tight I can't even feel my arms anymore when my dad comes bustling down the stairs.

"Bay, Bay, you're…you're okay!" he exclaims with tears in his eyes. I hug him too with my numb arms and then I hug them both at the same time. It felt so good to know that Eric was just trying to get under my skin, that everything was okay. And maybe he was dead, maybe this was all over. I don't even care, I have my family, Andrew, and my new friends, and I know that whatever happens, we'll do it together.

My parents don't even ask, I think they either don't want to pressure me, or make me relive it or whatever, but now we are basically inseparable. When I got to school, there was only twenty minutes left since my parents wanted me to get a lot of rest and food so I can stay healthy, and I can't argue with that logic.

I make it to school just in time to go to orchestra, I feel the vibrations, the message that the music is whispering to me, I feel like it's trying to tell me something important. I strain to hear from outside the door, I open it, and there sitting smack-dab in the middle is Andrew. I had planned what I would say to him the whole day. Would things go back to the way they were before we went to Roanoke, or would everything still be there?

I had no clue, but I realize my mouth is unnaturally dry, and for the first time in a long time, I go mute, feeling flustered and nervous. So without even batting my eyes, I conjure up a note that says everything it needed to. I slip it in his hand as I walk by feeling a spark of, of excitement? I hurry to my seat and watch him open it. I'm not sure what he thinks, but when he looks back at me, I give him thumb-up, basically bursting with joy. Everything was going to be okay. I think.

I go home and am just about ready for bed when the doorbell rings; I run down the stairs silently to the door. I unlock it, then take off the deadbolt, and finally turn the handle. I open the door expecting to see my parents, but there, standing tall and straight. His eyes fixed on me; he was wearing a fancy suit and holding something in his hand. *Oh god no!* I think.

"Hello, Bay Tine," says Eric Nova.

The End?

CPSIA information can be obtained at www.ICGtesting.com
Printed in the USA
LVOW12s0803021213

363499LV00032B/1009/P

9 781629 020471